pie in the sky

pie in the sky

Jane
Smiley

with illustrations by Elaine Clayton

ALFRED A. KNOPF
NEW YORK

THIS IS A BORZOI BOOK PUBLISHED BY ALFRED A. KNOPF

Visit us on the Web! randomhouse.com/kids

Educators and librarians, for a variety of teaching tools, visit us at
RHTeachersLibrarians.com

Library of Congress Cataloging-in-Publication Data
Smiley, Jane.
Pie in the Sky / Jane Smiley ; with illustrations by Elaine Clayton. — 1st ed.
    p. cm.
"A Borzoi Book."
ISBN 978-0-375-86968-6 (trade)—ISBN 978-0-375-96968-3 (lib. bdg.)—
ISBN 978-0-375-98532-4 (ebook)
[1. Horses—Training—Fiction. 2. Ranch life—California—Fiction.
3. High schools—Fiction. 4. Schools—Fiction. 5. Family life—California—Fiction.
6. Christian life—Fiction. 7. California—History—1950—Fiction.]
I. Clayton, Elaine, ill. II. Title.
PZ7.S6413Pie 2012
[Fic]—dc23
2011044104

The text of this book is set in 11.5-point Goudy.

Printed in the United States of America
September 2012
10 9 8 7 6 5 4 3 2 1
First Edition

pie in the sky

Straw Cowboy Hat

Sawcow

Chapter 1

ALL SUMMER LONG, MOM AND DAD TALKED ABOUT THE TEM-
perature. I would have thought that since they'd been living in
California now for nine years, they would have gotten used to
the weather, but no. It wasn't that they complained; it was that
they were always amazed. Now it was fifty, now it was seventy,
now it was a hundred, and all in the space of one day. In Oklahoma in the summer, it was always a hundred. That's what
they said.

No matter how hot it was at our place (and yesterday it was
a hundred), I knew to take a sweater when I went to the coast
to teach Melinda Anniston and Ellen Leinsdorf, which I did
every Saturday, even though my broken arm was healed and I
had plenty of horses to ride. There were several reasons to go—

Dad liked the income and experience for me, Mom liked the chance to do her shopping, and I liked both the girls and also their pony, Gallant Man, a pony that we had owned and sold to Melinda when her family had plenty of money, but that Ellen was now leasing half-time while the Annistons continued to fight about their divorce. This, Mom said, could take years. I also liked seeing Jane Slater, who always had something up her sleeve. Jane was neat and tidy every day, perfectly groomed and usually with a serious look on her face, but underneath that exterior was a person who liked to try things, and also liked me to try things, so when she came up to me after Ellen said good-bye and the groom, Rodney Lemon, took Gallant Man away to give him a bath, I knew she had a plan.

She said, "Oh, Abby, time to put in our entry blanks for the show next week."

"I thought we had to do that last week."

"Well, it is our show, so I reserve for myself the privilege of being a little late. Anyway, I've put both Ellen and Melinda in two classes. Melinda is in the two-foot pony hunters, one over fences and one on the flat, which I think she can do in one day without fainting from anxiety, and Ellen is in two walk-trot equitation classes, one on the flat and one over fences, but the fences are just cavalletti poles, hardly nine inches off the ground, just to teach the kids how to steer around a course."

"She could do more."

"But her mother couldn't stand it, so I think if her mother sees her do this, she'll be reassured and we can move forward at a brisker pace." She meant let Ellen do what she wanted to do, which was jump jump jump.

Jane looked me up and down. "Have you bought your boots yet?"

I nodded. Mom had finally given me permission to use some of the money I'd earned to buy a pair of black show boots, all the way to my knees, beautiful, soft, and gleaming, but she had made me buy them a size too large, in case I was still growing. I said, "I've been breaking them in for ten days."

"How do they feel?"

"Better. I can get my heels down now. Before, they were too stiff."

Jane nodded, then said, "I know you wanted them for a long time, and I always think they are the perfect example of a certain thing."

"What's that?"

"That getting what you want can be a little bit of a burden."

"I've already soaped them four times."

"There you go."

"But they look great."

She hugged me.

As we walked toward the parking lot, she said, "There's another thing."

"What's that?"

"Well, I talked Peter Finneran, the judge for the show, into staying an extra four days and giving a clinic after the show is over, and I want you to ride in it."

"What's a clinic?"

"That's when a famous equestrian gives three days of costly group lessons to those who sign up. It's very intensive, and you can learn a lot. Your trainers, who know you, might be overlooking things they ought to be seeing. The clinician picks them up. Peter Finneran is absolutely the most famous rider in the East now. Since we have him in California for a week, we need to keep him here and try to get some wisdom out of him. I already have trainers calling me from LA and San Francisco to sign up. I want you in there."

"On Blue?"

"Yes, you can take Blue."

"He's not jumping over three feet."

"That's fine for the first day anyway."

"How much is it?"

"I'll discuss that with your dad. I'll call him." We stopped. I could see Mom's car at the gate. Jane said, "Anyway, I put your name on Melinda's and Ellen's entry blanks as their trainer. You'll get paid for that," and she patted me on the shoulder and walked away, waving to Mom. I didn't know what to think, but then I never knew what to think when Jane came up with an idea.

Mom leaned over and gave me a peck on the cheek when I got into the car. "Here. I bought you an egg salad sandwich at the sandwich place beside the store. I know you have a lot to do this afternoon. It's downright chilly here and it was only seventy-four in town. I'm pretty sure it's cooled off at home." She handed me the sandwich. And a sugar cookie. And a bottle of Coke. She even had an opener to pop off the cap. We didn't have Cokes very often.

The first thing Mom did when we got home was check the temperature. She exclaimed, "Seventy-six! I thought so!" and went into the house after patting our dog, Rusty, on the head.

She slammed the door, and Rusty lay down on the porch and rolled over. I suppose she knew Mom was watching, because Mom then opened the door with a laugh and gave Rusty a dog biscuit.

You couldn't tell anymore that I had broken my arm almost five months earlier, falling off Danny's horse before she was Danny's horse—Happy, or Happily Ever After, which was her show name. Danny had just won two reining classes on her at the local rodeo. It was like they were welded together—whatever move she made, he was right with her. They hadn't gone in any roping classes, but I had seen Happy watching the calves. I imagined her slipping away and trotting over to where they were, saying, "Excuse me, excuse me. I have business over here. These calves need me."

My arm didn't hurt, and the bump that had been there when they took the cast off was gone. I had also built the muscles back up and both of my forearms looked the same now—a little brown and a little muscley. I made sure to work the left arm, the broken one, just a little more than the right one—to carry my books on the left, to open doors with the left, to carry my saddle on the left. Thinking about it reminded me to do the same for the horses—always work the weak side a little more than the strong side.

We had seven horses now. Amazon, Foxy, Jefferson, Sprinkles, and Happy had moved on, leaving Lincoln, Jack, and Blue. In June, Uncle Luke had brought us a full load, four mares: Lady, Morning Glory, Nobby, and Oh My. Oh My was a beautiful overo paint, black and white with one blue eye and a question mark on her shoulder. When people saw her, they said, "Oh my!" Daddy didn't expect to have her long. Nobby was a dark bay—Daddy thought she had some Tennessee Walker in her by the way she was built. She was very comfortable, even though Daddy hadn't asked her to "walk" yet. He rode her out because she was good at covering ground and very surefooted; "Couldn't resist" was all he said about her. Morning Glory was another pony ("Californians just love ponies!" he said), and I could ride her, but only just, and I hoped Daddy would sell her soon and then admit to himself that I was growing up. Lady was a lady—a bay quarter horse mare with a star shaped like a rectangle and the cowlick smack in the middle (you could measure it). She would make a good ranch horse, parade horse, whatever. In the old days, horses like Lady were the only ones Daddy really wanted to buy, because they were the most useful and easiest to sell, but after Black George and Gallant Man and Foxy, he had realized that Californians were different from Oklahomans—the stranger a horse was, the more they liked him or her. That afternoon, I was to ride Blue, Oh My, and Nobby, and also to work Jack in the pen. My real plan, since Daddy was in town and it was only seventy-six degrees, was to let Jack play around in the arena while I rode Blue.

I went straight to the barn, grabbed my saddle and Blue's bridle, took them over to the arena, and hung them on the fence. Blue worked in the arena four or five days a week—even though he had been afraid there when we first got him, he now was perfectly at home, and never flicked an ear at the cones or the poles lying along the fence line or the sawcow in the middle. Rusty could slip under the fence and run right in front of him and he didn't even sidestep.

First I got Jack—put on the halter and lead rope and made him walk along properly, about a foot behind my shoulder on my right side, with the rope loose between us. Every couple of steps I stopped suddenly, and he was supposed to pay attention and stop, too. Once I sped up to a fast walk, and he kept pace with me but didn't get excited or get ahead. He was eighteen months old now and knew to keep his eye on me and mind his manners. Most of the time he did what he was supposed to do, but not always. Daddy said he was "full of himself"; Jem Jarrow, our trainer, said he was "a character"; and Danny said he was "a real little man." I just thought he was a thing of beauty. I opened the gate and led him in, turned him, got him to make eye contact with me, then took off the halter. He paused for about one second and then leapt into the air with a squeal. I went back for Blue.

Blue was seven years old, a grown-up horse, but also, I was sure, a Thoroughbred. I myself had bought him on the spur of the moment from Jane after his previous owner died in a car accident. No one knew anything about him or about his previous owner, and for a while that had made me really nervous. He did not have a tattoo under his upper lip, which would show that he had raced, but he had the Thoroughbred look— elegant slim head, long legs, prominent withers—and he had a beautiful floating canter, wonderful to watch and even more wonderful to ride. Riding his canter put me in sort of a daze. I brought him into the arena, and while Jack sniffed cones and trotted around, I tacked Blue up and got on him. He looked at Jack sometimes, but his attitude seemed to be "Kids will be kids, but I have work to do."

I had him turn right and then left in a figure eight, then

around again. I reached for the right rein and had him lift his head to the right and step under, the way I always got my horses to loosen up and relax. He did that easily. Then he did it to the left. I sat a little deep in the saddle, shoulders up, elbows down, and asked him to back up. He tucked his chin and stepped backward, boom boom boom. Then I had him walk along the rail on a loose rein, with his head down and taking long, stretchy steps. Easy as pie. He sighed. He sighed again.

Jack was nosing under the fence for the dead grass and finding a little something—there are plenty of things that people call weeds that horses think taste good. Dad said that this is the way horses get vitamins and other nutrients—from all sorts of plants, not just grass. As usual for Jack, he was also watching; sometimes he watched us, and sometimes he looked over at the mares or Lincoln, and sometimes he looked up the hill. Rusty came out of the barn, and Jack stared at her for a minute; then she ambled over and sat by the gate, licking her paws.

I asked Blue to trot. He responded nicely. We did a serpentine to the end of the arena, four loops and back, four loops, and then two figure eights and an inward spiral. I made him move along but didn't push him too hard. Then I asked for the canter. A relaxed trot always gave me the urge to feel that canter. This time I made myself let him pick his own speed. He did. It was slow but smooth and easy. We went once around, turned left, crossed the center, where he changed leads, and went once around to the right. Jack noticed us and trotted here and there, snorting, but Blue ignored him. Finally, I took a deep breath, and he took this as an invitation to walk. We walked. I have to admit that I was not in the mood to do a lot of work, but Blue was perfect. Mostly I thought about how well he was going to do in the show, and how proud I would be to have him there, and how everyone would admire us.

Once I had brushed off Jack and Blue and put them away, I got on Oh My. Our only job for the day was to walk to the end of the fence line and then head up the hillside toward Mr. Jordan's place. Once we got there, we were to walk along his fence line with the barbed wire to our left. Then we were to turn and come back, keeping the wire to the right. The next exercise was to come down the hill—not straight down but in a long diagonal, then go up again, come down in the opposite diagonal, and then go up again and come straight down, me sitting back and Oh My using her hocks and haunches to steady herself. She was a beautiful horse, but to be useful on a ranch, she had to be able to handle the terrain. We did all of this at the walk. As she got into better condition, we would speed up. Nobby had to do the same thing. It wasn't hard, but I needed to pay attention, and by the time I was finished, I was sweaty and my hair was damp and flat against the top of my head, because Mom always made me wear a hard hat even though Dad and Danny wore straw cowboy hats in the summer, which were much cooler. I had once been allowed to wear a cowboy hat, too, but then Mom met Jane Slater, and that was that—hard hat for me.

On the front table was an envelope—covered with little pictures, only the address (to me) neatly framed by a white rectangle. The pictures were tiny faces—all the kids in our class, and recognizable, too. It was beautiful, but I was not happy to receive it. The party I was being invited to was a farewell party for the Goldman twins, who had decided to go to boarding school and would be leaving after the horse show—first for a vacation to New York City, and then to their school, which was down in Los Angeles, or, as Barbie said, "in the wilds of Malibu." I could not get a straight answer about this school from either Barbie or Alexis. Supposedly, they would be living in tents and digging wells and planting their own potatoes and turnips and earning their keep by playing duets (violin and piano) on the streets of Santa Monica, and it was a good thing that I had taught Barbie to ride a horse, because that way, when they rode horses down there, which they had to do, she could tell Alexis what to do every minute of the day. "It's too late, she had her chance, and I beat her to it. It was horses or banjo, and she chose banjo, and now I'm the boss." I was sure that Alexis would see things differently.

Mom and Dad had already agreed to let me go to the party, even though it might run late, and I knew it would be a good party, with strange but delicious food and activities that no one else in our class would ever think of. I opened the envelope very carefully, preserving all of the portraits. It was not like I didn't have other friends—I spent more time with Gloria and Stella than I did with the Goldmans (since they had so much music practice every day), but they could not be replaced by regular kids—that much I knew for sure.

Black Riding Jacket

Hard Hat

Chapter 2

THE HORSE SHOW ALWAYS RAN FROM WEDNESDAY TO SUNDAY. During the school year, I had shown on Saturday and Sunday, but that was when I had a champion horse and we knew what we were doing. Now we were starting out again, so we showed up on the much more quiet and relaxed days of Wednesday and Thursday, when the jumps were low. One thing about a horse show is that you can't pick and choose when your classes are going to be. I would have preferred Ellen one day, Melinda the next, and Blue and me on day three. But Melinda's classes came on Wednesday, at eight and eight thirty, Ellen's were at nine and nine forty-five, and I would have to be on Blue by eleven. We took Blue Tuesday afternoon, and found him a stall in the show barns, which were temporary canvas buildings set up in the polo field. Once I'd started riding him again after my broken arm had healed, we had taken him back to the stables twice for lessons with Jane. He seemed comfortable, but after all, he'd lived there for several months before I got him. The temporary stall had a bale of straw in it, which I spread around while Mom held Blue. Then I tacked him up and went out to have a lesson with Jane in the arena where we would be showing. We didn't jump very much, just walked, trotted, and cantered around, looking at the other horses, the tents, the jumps, the grooms, and cars and trucks going from place to place. I did a lot of stepping over and coming under, and this seemed to calm him. We left him at about six, with plenty of hay to eat, two full buckets of water, and him wearing one of his blankets because it was damp and chilly. Jane said she would check on him before leaving for the night.

Rodney Lemon was helping me with Gallant Man, but I was on my own with Blue—the show fees for the stall and the classes were pretty expensive, and since Blue had cost me all of $5.60 and Dad wasn't charging me for board or hay, he thought it would be a good lesson in money management for me to pay for the show out of what I had earned teaching Ellen, Melinda, and Barbie during the spring and summer. I had decided that I didn't want to pay Rodney to do what I could do myself; when I got up at four on Wednesday morning, I regretted that. Even so, I was pretty proud of how I looked, which was just like all the other riders—well-fitting tall black boots, canary (that's yellow) breeches, a clean white shirt, a black coat, black gloves, a stock, and my hard hat. Jane had loaned me the stock and helped me find the jacket and the breeches—she knew all sorts of college girls who had given up riding and were willing to sell their old clothes. I got the jacket for ten dollars and the breeches for twelve, about two weeks' worth of lessons. Even with the boots and the entry fees, I still had over a hundred dollars in my account at the bank, whether or not Dad permitted me to spend it.

I could not help looking around for Sophia Rosebury, whose outfits were always perfect and whose boots, Jane said, were custom made, but of course she would not be there on a Wednesday. Both of her horses were champions, and her horse Onyx, whom we used to call Black George when we owned him, was probably going to be Horse of the Year at these shows—he hardly ever lost, and I had to admit that it was because in addition to the fact that he loved to jump and was very easy to ride, Sophia hardly ever made a mistake. She was not a nice girl—for one thing, she never smiled—but she rode perfectly, as far as I could tell, and I watched her whenever I could. I sometimes wondered if she knew who I was or remembered that she had bought my horse, but I didn't say anything.

I checked on Blue and gave him some more hay, then went to the barns, where Melinda, of course, was waiting for me. She was standing with Rodney and Gallant Man, and Rodney had braided both the pony's mane and his tail, putting little red bows on every braid; they looked wonderful against Gallant Man's sparkling dapples. Melinda was frowning, with a straight line going right down between her eyebrows, and as soon as she saw me she said in a serious voice, "Hi, Abby. I've decided that it is best if I don't do this. It really is for the best."

I cleared my throat and pretended that I was considering

her opinion. Then I said, "Well, Melinda, why don't you get on Gallant Man, since he looks so great with the red braids, and we'll talk about it. We can walk over to the warm-up and you can at least watch."

"Right you are, then, miss!" exclaimed Rodney in his English accent, and he hoisted her into the saddle.

Melinda picked up the reins, and said, "Why—"

Rodney turned his back and walked away. Melinda looked after him.

I said, "Wow, Rodney really put a lot of braids in the pony's mane. I wonder how many?" I started walking, and Melinda followed me. She said, "Seventeen."

"Are you kidding? I don't believe you."

"Yes, seventeen."

I shook my head.

She started counting, and by the time we got to the ring, she was saying, "See? Seventeen, eighteen with the forelock."

"Have you patted your pony ten times today?"

She started patting.

"What time did you get here?"

"Well, May got me up at five, because I asked her to, but really, I couldn't open my eyes until almost five twenty because last night I was reading *Black Beauty*, and then I got to the part where Ginger dies and I started to cry, so I stayed up sort of late."

By this time, I was walking into the warm-up ring. Melinda was talking and following me. I said, "That is sad. I cried there, too. Okay, why don't you just trot around me in a nice circle and we can see how Gallant Man feels this morning."

She was going before she realized it, and then she was fine. Melinda was always more scared of things in advance and afterward than she was while she was doing them. But she had grown, at long last. She was eleven now, and I wasn't sure how much longer she would look good on Gallant Man. I put that out of my mind, because it wasn't any of my business.

Since we were early, there were only three other riders in the warm-up. All the girls were courteous and looking out for each other, and I saw that they were careful to pass "left hand to left hand," which is how, when you are approaching another horse and rider, you know who goes to the outside and who goes to the inside. They were all also looking at each other— who had the prettier horse or pony? What were they all wearing? That was something Melinda cared about, so as she lifted her chin and showed off a little, she got less nervous.

There were three plain jumps across the middle of the warm-up, just standards and poles. The crossbar was to the left, the oxer to the right, and the regular jump in the middle. As Melinda headed down toward the crossbar for the first time, I saw Jane show up near the gate of the warm-up with Mr. Anniston. She was talking; he wasn't saying anything. Melinda trotted down toward the crossbar, cantered the last two strides, and jumped it nicely, then cantered away, smiling. I hoped she wouldn't see her father. I shouted, "Okay, very nice, come around and do it again." She did, and still did not see her father. I pointed her toward the regular jump, which was maybe two feet. She had to pause and wait for the girl on the palomino, and when she did, she saw her father. The palomino went over. Gallant Man slowed his trot and stopped. Melinda caught herself. I called out, "Try again. Give him a kick and make sure he's going. *You* have to want to jump, or he won't care."

Jane stared at Melinda, then me. Then she took the hint and walked away with Mr. Anniston. I hoped she would keep him off in a corner for the whole morning. I had never seen him smile. Melinda and Gallant Man made a little circle and went back to the jump. Two strides out, she gave him a kick, and of course he bounced over, easy as you please. He didn't look very good—his front legs weren't neatly folded—but when she came around again, he sorted himself out and did a good job. Then they jumped the oxer twice, and both times perfectly. When I took Melinda to the gate of the show ring, she had an unusual look on her face—a look of determination. I realized that part of Melinda's problem was that Gallant Man never made a mistake, and so she never really understood that she was in charge. Now she did.

It was time to walk the course. I wasn't sure what to do with Gallant Man, but then a groom for the girl on the bay held out his hand, and the girl said, "Andy will hold your pony, if I can walk the course with you." She jumped down. I said, "Okay."

The course was eight jumps, two turns. Simple enough until jump seven, when the girls had to turn away from the jump that came eight strides after number six and roll back to the right, toward another that was more or less behind them— the clue was that number six was a little brush, and number seven was a little brush. The one they were not supposed to jump was a chicken coop. I pointed this out, and they both nodded. Then we stood in the center of the ring, and I made them do my favorite thing—hold one of their hands up and walk their fingers around the course while reciting the numbers. After they were done, I said, "Do you know it?" Melinda nodded, and the girl said, "It's easy."

I said, "We'll see." There were a lot of jumps in the ring. I would have found it confusing. We went back to the horses. Andy handed me Gallant Man. I said, "Are you the groom?"

He laughed, and said, "No, I'm the brother. We don't have a groom or a trainer, just us."

The girl said, "I'm Daphne." Andy gave her a leg up onto the bay. I wondered where they had come from, since I'd never seen them before, but I forgot about them as soon as I saw Mr. Anniston go into the tent by the ring and sit down on one of the benches. I wished Jane would put a bag over his head. Okay, with holes cut out so he could see.

But Melinda was so focused on remembering the course that she didn't notice him. She waited for her number to be called, and when it was, she trotted in and made her circle. She did just what I'd told her—she veered as close as she could to some of the jumps, so that Gallant Man could see them (actually, so that Melinda could see them; Gallant Man didn't care). And after a long minute and twenty seconds, they came out, having done a pretty good job. At least he went straight to the fences, and Melinda's position was good. Daphne went after them. She was very good. But Melinda didn't care—she got a ribbon (fourth out of six), and she had taken the whole course by herself without making a mistake. She was grinning. Daphne continued to be nice—back in the warm-up, she called out, "Good job!"

Melinda said, "You too!"

I guessed that Daphne was also eleven, but she seemed older and more self-confident.

In the flat class, Melinda went around nicely, not quite showing off enough, but evidently happy. She smiled at Daphne every time she saw her, and Daphne smiled back. Daphne got second, and Melinda got third. Rodney met us at the gate. He had Ellen by the hand. Melinda jumped down and ran over to her dad, brandishing her ribbon. He still didn't smile, but he patted her on the head. That was the last I saw of them, because Ellen was ready to mount up and go. Rodney didn't give her a leg up—he picked her up and sat her on the pony. She grabbed the reins, and Gallant Man tossed his head. I said, "Ellen, remember what I said about holding him too tightly. He doesn't like it."

She loosened her reins.

I said, "Take a deep breath. Or two."

She took two deep breaths.

I said, "Pat the pony."

She put both her reins in her right hand and patted the pony. This was something we did at every lesson.

Ellen was tough and often angry, but if you told her what to do in a way that she understood, she would do it. As we were walking into the warm-up, I said, "Don't show off. It makes you put your heels down too far and arch your back too much. Just try to pay attention to your pony and make it easy for him." This was her first show. I had no idea what would happen. In the warm-up, I had her practice walk, trot, and canter, since the first class was the flat class.

There were five kids in the group, four girls and one boy. They looked about eight, except for the boy, who looked about six. Their ponies were all tried and true—way older than their riders. The other trainers were standing here and there, shouting commands: "Lift your eyes, Rachel! Look where you're going!" "Ginny, heels down! Good girl." "Robert, shorten your reins!" The announcer called the class.

Ellen came over to me and took a deep breath, which made her nostrils flare, and tossed her head, which made her braids bounce. She said, "I'm ready."

She was. She walked into the ring ahead of all the others and turned right, walking along the rail, urging Gallant Man. He went at such a brisk pace, I thought he might trot, but he didn't. Her reins were short, but then she noticed and loosened them. I whispered, "Good girl." The kids were told to trot.

I won't say that all the ponies wandered around the ring the whole time, but it was pretty chaotic, and twice ponies came close to the back of the black pony with two white hind feet, who pinned his ears and looked like he might kick. But Ellen and Gallant Man stayed out of trouble, stopped when told to, trotted when told to, turned when told to, and trotted out when told to. Ellen wasn't bad at steering, either. It was clear that she and one other girl, Ginny, who was on a bay pony mare, were the best, but the judge let them go around for a while, I suppose to get practice. Finally, he called them into the center and gave Ginny the blue ribbon and Ellen the red ribbon. Ellen came out of the ring in a snit, but her mother appeared right there and said, "Oh, darling, how wonderful! You were so good! I am proud of you!" She had some sugar cubes, which she handed to Ellen, and with all of that, Ellen relaxed, gave the pony the sugar, and didn't have a tantrum.

The practice ring was now set with three cavalletti poles. These are poles that have X's nailed to each end, and they can be jumps of different heights depending on how you turn the X's. When the pole is turned downward, the jump is about six inches. When the pole is on its side, the jump is about nine inches, and when it's turned upward, about twelve inches. Ellen was secretly jumping about eighteen inches in our lessons, and Gallant Man could easily do three feet, so we only practiced a couple of times in the warm-up, and then went first into the ring. The point was steering. Ellen was good at steering, since she knew always to look ahead. I didn't think I had ever seen her look down.

She did what I had told her—made a little circle, then trotted around the course. The course was two cavalletti, then a left turn away from the rail and back over the same two, then around the end of the ring and down over two that were set diagonally through the center, then around to the right and down over the last two, halting at the end, turning, and trotting over the last one going the other way, and then making another small circle. Her first loop was a little big, and she veered a little to the right on the last jump, but I was pleased with her.

Ginny did well, too, with just one mistake—breaking to the walk before the third jump, but only for a stride. The other kids were chaos. Robert's trainer finally had to go in, after he had come to a halt facing the judge's stand, and lead him over the last four cavalletti. Robert was crying. Ellen stood beside

Gallant Man and stared at every one of the other children. I would have said she was casting a spell on them, if I believed in spells.

As soon as the announcer said, "And a tie for first place goes to Ellen Leinsdorf and Virginia Cartwright, on—" Ellen was away from me, leading Gallant Man and running into the ring. Gallant Man trotted after her, his ears flicking. I said, "Hey!" but they were gone. Ellen was shouting, "What about the jump-off? There should be a jump-off!" The announcer stopped speaking. In the silence, Ellen sounded even louder. She wasn't screaming, but she did have a loud voice. "In the program it says there will be a jump-off!" Since I hadn't read the program, I didn't know that this was true, but in some things Ellen was never wrong. I got to her and took Gallant Man's reins. Jane came hurrying into the arena. Ellen began to scowl, and I started to worry—once in the spring when she saw that she wasn't going to get her way, she'd thrown herself right off the pony, flat on the ground.

But then the judge nodded and the announcer said, "The judge says that there will be a jump-off between Virginia Cartwright and Ellen Leinsdorf. Girls, please come to the judge's stand and listen to your course." Jane and I exchanged a glance, and then Ginny came over with her trainer, and we all listened.

The judge was not Peter Finneran, just a man from San Francisco who often did the lower-level classes. He was tall and blond and wore an ascot—this morning it was red—but he seemed pretty nice. He told the girls that since a jump-off was supposed to be shorter and faster than the class, they were to do the first four jumps again, down, around in a loop, then back over the jumps, but this time at the canter rather than the trot. The girls nodded. They would go alphabetically, Ginny first. We all walked out of the ring.

I gave Ellen a leg up.

Ginny entered, trotted, began a little circle, and turned toward the jumps. She kicked the pony and he picked up a nice canter, then went over the two cavalletti. As they came over the second one, I saw that she had lucked out—her pony landed on the left lead, which meant that she only had to make her loop and come back and she would be correct. This is what happened, and they finished jumps three and four very neatly, coming down to a trot circle, and exiting the arena.

I said to Ellen, "Okay. We haven't talked much about leads, but you know the difference. It doesn't matter what lead he's on to begin with, but he has to be on the left lead for that loop, so if he lands on the right lead, trot and fix it, because he doesn't like the left lead, and he might not take that lead by himself."

She nodded. She went in, made a nice circle, picked up the canter, and headed for the jump. I thought his jumps were nicer than the other pony's. But he did land on the right lead, it did take Ellen a few strides to notice, and when she changed it, Gallant Man looked a little awkward. They ended up with second after all.

But I had to hand it to Ellen—when I asked her what she'd learned from this whole episode, she said, "To get him better on the left lead." This made me chuckle for the rest of the morning.

24

Daddy was brushing Blue. My jacket and my stock were hanging on the bridle hook with my hard hat. In two minutes or so, Blue was tacked up and I was dressed and mounted on him, still thinking about Ellen and Melinda. This was a mistake, since I was too distracted to notice that Blue was tight and nervous, and when we came out of the aisle of the temporary barns and to the railing of the warm-up, he saw one of the tents flutter, and spooked. He almost had me off. I grabbed his mane. Daddy came up behind us and said, "What was that?"

I said, "Must have been a ghost."

But I knew it was the tent. I sat up straight and pushed my heels down, and paid attention; he remained nervous. A moment later, Jane showed up. She had a lunge line. All of a sudden I remembered that I had a trainer, too—Jane. I was really glad to see her.

We walked, Jane in front and Dad behind, past all the rings and tents and food places, to the farthest warm-up, where you were allowed to lunge. The fog had lifted and evaporated, and the light on the horses and the tents was bright the way it gets when there is still some moisture in the air that makes everything sparkly. The temperature was about perfect, too—cool enough if you were wearing a black jacket and tall boots, but not making your cheeks freeze. At the farthest arena, I dismounted, and Jane ran the snap of the lunge line through the inside ring of Blue's bit and attached it to the outside one. She stepped into the middle, and Dad and I stood by the fence. Blue went around and around, first trotting, then cantering. I would have preferred a round corral, just because I liked him to turn and go the other way as many times as possible—my trainer, Jem Jarrow, said that just the turning loosened their backs. But the thing about a horse show is that you have to do it their way, not your way. That's part of the test. Same with a rodeo.

Blue must have gone around twenty times—it was like he didn't know how to be tired. Daddy said, "Must be more nervous than we thought."

I also thought he was nervous, but I said, "Why?"

"A nervous horse, especially a nervous-type horse, doesn't really know when he's tired or when he's had too much. He's running on fizz. Maybe he'll calm down."

Jane stopped him, turned him, and switched the lunge line, and then they started again, first trotting and then cantering. His canter was beautiful, as always, just his body opening and closing. But it was Jane who had to stop him—he didn't think of it himself. Dad said, "Thoroughbred through and through," shaking his head as if that were a bad thing. He gave me a leg up, and Blue and I followed Jane to the warm-up ring. Of the ten entries in our class, five had gone already. As soon as we got into the warm-up, I trotted around once, and then Jane pointed me down over the crossbar.

Well, I was worse than either Melinda or Ellen. I didn't know why. I could walk around, trot around, canter, and jump, and I could see the things I was doing wrong—leaning forward with my shoulders, letting my hands drop and my heels come up, not being in the center of my horse—but it was like my brain was hardly working. Twice over the crossbar, and two bad jumps, one with me too far forward and one with me left behind. I felt like Blue was saying, "Who is this riding me?" I bought him to a halt, sat up, and took some deep breaths. Then I pushed my heels down, settled my shoulders, and cantered down to the regular jump, not the crossbar. He went over it nicely.

And they were calling my number from the show ring. As we left the warm-up, Jane put her hand on my boot. She said, "A green horse is a challenge, but you've done all of these things before, and he can do it. He needs some hand-holding. Every green horse does. But you're good at hand-holding, and he trusts you. Just stay with him and make him go forward." I didn't have time to ask him to step under, even once, before we were in the ring, making our circle. And even though the course was the same as Melinda's course had been, and even though I had walked it and thought about it and walked my fingers over it, I did not know where I was going, or maybe even who I was.

We finished the circle, and I asked Blue for the canter. He took the proper lead, but then when I steered him down toward the first fence, which was a small coop, you would have thought I was asking him to jump off a building. His ears went forward and I could feel his weight shift backward as he got ready to stop. However, I kicked him and he jumped awkwardly. But we had jumped coops dozens of times. Then came the next fence, just some plain white poles. He didn't try to stop, but he took off in the next county somewhere, and our jump was broad and flat. Now we had a turn. I remembered not to lean into the turn, so I was sitting up straight for the next jump, which was a good thing, because it felt like he jumped the way a deer jumps, all four legs stiff and bounding off the ground. After jump four, I sort of gave up on the course and turned him in a circle. I sat up and took a deep breath, shook my shoulders, and kicked him. I even said out loud, "You gotta do it, Blue. And you can." I sat deep in the saddle. The last four jumps were okay, though I had no idea what leads we were on. We survived, but we did not jump like we knew what we were doing. When we came down to the trot, I thought of how that boy Robert felt, crying in front of the judge and having to be led out.

Daddy had sort of a dumbstruck look on his face, and Jane was shaking her head, if only just a little. She patted Blue on the shoulder and said, "Well, the next class will be an improvement, I'm sure."

That kid Andy, who was riding an Appaloosa, won the class. He waved to me as he was coming out of the ring with his ribbon, which I at first thought was sort of mean, but then when I looked back at him, he had such a friendly smile on his face that I decided he didn't know how bad I had been—maybe he had been doing something else when I was having my round. I walked Blue slowly back to the barn. The clock, when I passed it, was at 11:35. Surely, I thought, that would be p.m., given how exhausted I was.

Daddy had gone to get the truck and trailer, since we were taking Blue home for the night. Our classes Thursday weren't until the afternoon. After I untacked Blue, brushed him off a little and put him in the stall, I took off my jacket and stock, and then my boots. They were a little muddy and would have to be cleaned again that night. I yawned. Then I yawned again. I really, really hoped that there was nothing weird going on at home—last fall we'd gotten back from a horse show, and Mr. Jordan's blue Brahma cows and calves had broken through the fence up the hill and come all the way down to our place, looking for hay, most likely.

But everything was quiet, though hot—ninety at least, and now I was thinking like Mom and Dad.

Scraper

Brush

Chapter 3

BECAUSE I HAD GONE TO BED BEFORE EIGHT, I WAS UP BEFORE six. Daddy had already left for Modesto, where he was going to look at a horse. Mom had made a coffeecake and was in her room getting dressed. While I was eating my second piece, Danny showed up and said that he would ride everyone that day because he had a day off from his job shoeing horses for Jake Morrison, and after he got everyone ridden, he would drive Blue and me out to the stable, and then go to a beach party with Leah, who wasn't really his girlfriend, but they did do things. He said, "I guess you're going to miss Barbie and Alexis." Leah was Barbie and Alexis's cousin. She was nice, but much quieter than they were.

"Barbie said they have to play music on the streets of Santa Monica to earn money for the school."

Danny said, "Do you believe everything you hear?"

"I don't believe that Leah is not your girlfriend."

"Well, she's going to Berkeley in a week, so girlfriend or not, it doesn't matter."

I stared at him. But he was being Danny. You couldn't tell what he thought, really.

After breakfast, I cleaned my boots and polished them again. They did feel comfortable now—I couldn't blame my bad round on them. I didn't know what to blame it on, except hurry. Today, I was not going to hurry. Danny would be at the beach party until four, and my job, after my classes, was to eat a hot dog, drink a Coke, and relax until he got back. Blue and I were going to take our time, including around the courses.

Danny wasn't much of a talker, so as we drove along, I had to think my own thoughts, and about every other thought had to do with the feeling I'd had the day before of knowing what was wrong with my riding but not being able to do anything about it. As we got closer to the stable, those thoughts got to be two out of three and then three out of four. When we pulled into the parking lot, the sun was just out and the day was half bright and half foggy. I felt like I was paying a visit to yesterday. I sighed. Danny turned off the truck engine and put his hand on my arm. He said, "Look ahead. Look ahead. You just go around the course and with every stride, you say, 'Look ahead. Look ahead.'" I nodded.

Blue backed out of the trailer, lifted his head, pricked his ears, and whinnied long and loud, and of course I thought he was saying, "Are we here again? Oh no!" Another horse whinnied in response. I wished I could think he was saying hi, but I thought he was saying, "Go away." Danny gave me a little punch on the arm, and as I turned to lead Blue toward the row of stalls, I said, "Say hi to Leah for me."

I put Blue in the stall with a large flake of oat hay and a bucket of water, and went to look for Jane. I found her at the main arena, the one with the big tent and the big jumps and the big announcer's stand. She was leaning on the fence, talking to that boy Andy. He saw me before she did, and smiled. Jane turned around. She said, "Oh, Abby, you're here! Today is another day, right?"

I said, "Right."

Andy said, "You have that gray horse, don't you?"

"Blue."

"He's a beauty. Daphne and I were admiring him."

I said, "I can't imagine when."

He laughed in a way that let me know he had seen my course. That was depressing.

Gloria and Stella would not have said that Andy was a cute boy, but that was because he didn't look like the boys in our class. I now saw that even though he was only an inch taller than I, he was Danny's age for sure. He had bowlegs, like Danny, and big hands, and he was missing one tooth. But another way that he wasn't like the boys in our class was that he didn't seem to care about these things—he smiled and looked happy anyway. Jane seemed to like him—she gave him one of those grown-up looks that said, "Such a nice young man!" Then she told him, "Well, you did an excellent job in that class this morning. That was a twisty course."

"Rascal is pretty handy. But Dad's made him handier. You know how Dad is."

Jane laughed. "Yes, I do. If anyone is going to teach a horse to do backflips, it's going to be your dad."

"It's not like he hasn't tried."

They both laughed. Then Jane said, "Well, let's have a look at Blue today. Since he was turned out last night, maybe he won't be so wound up. I am at your service, because all the little girls are home for the day."

Once we had left the arena, I asked Jane, "Who is that kid?"

"Oh, Andy? Andy Carmichael. His dad has a place up near Santa Rosa, but he started out in gold country—over by Placerville somewhere. Ralph Carmichael. He is famous."

"For what?"

"Oh, goodness. Well, I guess he's most famous for that horse Auburn. Auburn was headed for the slaughter, and Ralph was driving by the yard, the way he often did, and saw Auburn. He went in and bought him for ten dollars, took him home and fed him up, and taught him to jump. But Auburn couldn't really be ridden. He would buck even Ralph off, so he got him to jump as part of an act that he used to take to fairs up there. He would park six cars in the arena, and send Auburn around and Auburn would jump over all the cars, first one direction and then the other. There were some other horses in the show, too. Ralph jumped a course on one of them standing up on its back. Ralph will do anything." She lowered her voice. "Colonel Hawkins does not approve." Colonel Hawkins was Jane's boss. He ran the stable and had been in the cavalry. He was very upright and serious.

34

I said, "They are good riders. His sister was in Melinda's class."

"Oh, yes. They're good. I guess they have a couple of horses they want to show around for sale as jumpers. Andy says he's taking the Appy in a few bigger classes. Yesterday and today are just practice for Saturday. Ralph is arriving then."

We walked along.

"They do this on their own?"

"Not completely. Ralph is somewhere not too far away. But Andy is a very responsible kid."

We came to the ring where my class would be, and looked at the map of the course. It was suspiciously simple—basically a figure eight, with the addition of a line of three jumps at the end, and then a turn to the last one, a brush. We went in and walked it, then I walked my fingers around it. Fortunately, the jumps we would be jumping were the only ones in the arena, so I didn't have to worry about the thing I always worried about, which was seeing something and jumping it when it wasn't even part of the course (I had never actually done this). All the jumps in a course have a number in front of them, but I ask you, can you tell as you are galloping down to a fence whether the red number on a white background is the one for your class, or whether it's the blue number on a yellow background? Every course at a horse show was a test. I learned it as well as I could, and we headed back to the show barns.

Blue had finished his hay and was looking through the bars of the temporary stall. He whinnied to us when we approached. Jane helped me clean him up. We brushed his legs and ran a cloth all over him. When we had him out of the stall, we wiped his mouth, combed his forelock, and got all the grit off his hooves. I put the saddle and bridle on, and then Jane held him while I put on my coat and hard hat. Once I had mounted, using the mounting block, she polished my boots with a rag.

She said, "Did you lunge him at home?"

"I put him in the round corral and made him work for a pretty long time."

"He seems a little more relaxed today."

But as we got closer to the arena, I got more nervous, and then I felt him get more nervous. I felt like Melinda when I said, "I don't think I can do this."

"Abby Lovitt!" She spun around and looked up at me. "What am I hearing?"

"Well, it was sort of hard when I was riding Black George, because I wasn't always sure I knew my way around the course. But if I got there, he would always jump it. Now I have two things—where to go and how to help Blue. I don't know if I can do two things."

Jane nodded. "Yes. You're right. You have exactly those two things. But everyone in the ring has something or other."

Just then, Sophia Rosebury walked by, sitting on her chestnut, whose name was Pie in the Sky, which I thought was a silly name. She went by without even looking in our direction. After a moment, I said, "What does Sophia Rosebury have?" I may have sounded a little snotty.

Jane looked up at me. "Sophia Rosebury is a perfectionist. Do you know what that is?"

I nodded.

"Well, being a perfectionist seems okay from the outside, but a perfectionist never enjoys anything, no matter how well it goes, because nothing is ever perfect. And a horse, believe me, is one of those things that is never ever going to be perfect."

"Black George is perfect."

She stopped and put her hand on Blue's shoulder. She said, "To us, Onyx is perfect. But if you are a perfectionist, the better things are, the more dissatisfied you get with tiny things that no one else will notice."

"That's like my friend Stella and her outfits."

"She has nice clothes?"

"Beautiful ones."

"Would you trade being yourself with your clothes for being her with her clothes?"

I shook my head.

"Well, there you go. Okay, trot him with the others in here. He finds other horses reassuring. It should loosen him up a bit if you weave around without getting in anyone else's way."

I saw that she had done to me what I did to Melinda—talk about something so that you don't notice what you are doing until you are doing it. I smiled.

I wove carefully among the ten or twelve horses and riders in the warm-up. I lifted the rein in the direction I was turning Blue toward, and I could feel his shoulder and his back curve and his inside hind leg step further underneath himself, and almost without being able to help it, he got looser and smoother. After a couple of minutes, he blew air out of his nostrils, also a good sign. Horses can't hold their breath, but they do breathe more shallowly or more deeply. When they are breathing more deeply, they are happier.

I began to notice other riders looking at him. Was Blue the most beautiful horse I had ever seen? What I liked about Blue was that everything about him seemed to flow, even when he was just standing there. He could not do a single thing, including taking a drink of water, that wasn't beautiful—if he was taking a drink of water, his neck arched, and you had to admire the way his throat came into his cheek. And, to tell the truth, there is nothing like a gray, especially a dappled gray with a black mane and tail, which was what Blue was. Yes, someday, when he was fifteen or twenty, he would be white, but now his bluish dappling looked like a painting all over his body, the sort of painting that made all his curves stand out. Other riders looking at him reminded me of my fantasy—that we would be admired. I sat up a little straighter.

Once we had woven our way around the warm-up at the walk, trot, and canter, Jane set the crossbar fairly low, and I brought Blue around in a big circle to jump it. I looked at the jump. I looked past the jump. I felt him shift his weight backward again, and my heart popped, but I closed my legs and he went over it. We cantered on, came around, and did it again. Jane raised the ends, making a steeper X, and he jumped a little higher and more carefully. I began to relax. We jumped the regular jump and then the oxer. We wandered around the warm-up and went over to look at the other horses in the ring. I took a lot of deep breaths. I patted my horse. I shook out my shoulders. I went back into the warm-up for one last, easy canter.

What is the opposite of a perfectionist? For a perfectionist, everything goes as well as possible, and still there's something to worry about or complain about. The opposite of a perfectionist is someone who refuses the first jump, then jumps it, but awkwardly, trots to the second jump instead of cantering, jumps that one awkwardly, then knocks a top pole from the third jump and two poles from the fourth jump, an oxer. Finally, she misses the fifth jump entirely, and when the buzzer sounds to tell her she is off course, she makes a circle and jumps up onto the bank, but only by mistake—the bank isn't on the course. It is right beside the judge's stand.

I looked the judge right in the eye (this time it was Peter Finneran), and I knew he thought we were going to run right over him. We stood there, Blue and I. Then, after three deep breaths, we got down from the bank and left the arena. That's the opposite of a perfectionist, and it makes being a perfectionist look pretty good. Jane only said, "Well, your position was excellent. That's a positive thing."

We walked back to the warm-up, and I could tell Jane was thinking about the best thing to do with me. On the one hand, you don't want your last experience of the day to be a disaster, but on the other hand, it could get worse. I thought about Jem Jarrow—what would he say? And I decided that he would say, "Never be too lazy to get off your horse and do some ground work." I said to Jane, "How long till the next class?"

"Well, it starts in twenty minutes, but it's a big class. It could go a half an hour or more."

I halted Blue, took my feet out of the stirrups, and jumped off. I said, "I think I would like to take him somewhere quiet and do some ground work."

"Do you mind if I go have some lunch while you're doing that?"

In fact, I preferred it.

She pointed me to the lunging area, and we parted. I looked at Blue as we were walking through the riders and horses and trainers and dogs on leashes and said, "Are you making me nervous, or am I making you nervous? I wish I knew."

We walked along. Blue looked here and there, his ears pricking but not arrowing forward. He blew out some air. He lifted his head and put it down again. We came to the lunging ring, and it was empty. I unfastened one rein from his bit, so that I had a longish line, and I stood beside his head, facing backward, one hand on the rein down by the bit and the other on his shoulder. Then I lifted the rein so that his head turned and came up, and I pressed a little bit on his shoulder. He curved away from me. I didn't push him or cluck to him or anything; I just waited. Finally, he stepped the hind foot on that side underneath his body and across the other hind foot, and his body curled away from me. I did it again and again, and after a few times, we had made a little tiny circle, and were facing the same direction again. Then I let the rein slide through my hand and also lifted my crop. He moved forward, then away from me, curving his body and stepping around me. He did this twice, and then I had him walk and then trot in a tiny circle, making sure that he was stepping under and under and under. His mouth was soft. Then I did all of these things on the other side. Then I had him back up. I said, "Back!" and he started backing. He could have backed all the way to the railing, no problem. It wasn't that he didn't want to do what I wanted him to do.

I attached the rein and tightened the girth, then mounted him. We did all these same exercises with me on his back, and

I would have said that he was ready for anything, so I turned him toward a little jump that was set up in the middle—really not more than two feet. About four strides out from the jump, I could feel his weight shift. I could see his ears go up. He did go over the jump, but awkwardly. I thought maybe he just wasn't a jumper, but then I thought, How could a horse with such a beautiful canter and gallop not be able to jump? A jump is just a big canter stride—that's what Black George would say. Then Jane appeared and waved me to the regular warm-up. As I was passing her, she looked up at me and said, "Don't forget to ride the course, not the jumps."

That was exactly what I had forgotten to do. When I was first riding with Jane, I had made a list of rules for jumping, and Daddy and I would go over them almost every day. They were: ride the course (not the jumps), keep the horse level (especially through the turns), look ahead ten strides (not two or five), ride to the middle of every fence, wait (or don't hurry, but I guess it's better to think about what you should do than about what you shouldn't do), maintain a rhythm in your canter, and look up (never down).

I could recite these in my sleep, so it was amazing that I was breaking so many rules riding these jumps. I mean, these courses. In the warm-up ring, with Jane watching, I made myself concentrate on looking ahead ten strides, and we got over all of the practice fences pretty well. At least Jane said, "Much better, Abby!"

I watched the second-to-last rider go, and walked my fingers along with her around the course. I was concentrating on my fingers. I could not have told you anything about the rider.

Then I went into the arena. I said to myself, over and over, "Ride the course, not the jumps." We did our circle. Blue took the proper lead, and we headed down to the first jump. Four strides out, he shifted his weight backward and arrowed his ears at the fence. I could feel him looking right at it, his nose tipping downward as we got closer, and I said aloud, "Look ahead Blue. Look at the next jump." I even lifted his nose a little with the reins, and kicked him on. He jumped the fence and headed for number two. This time, as we approached the jump (a triple bar), I said, "Look around the turn, Blue. The next fence is around the turn." We jumped the fence, staying level, and that third fence wasn't out of my sight until it was time to look ahead to the fourth fence. And so it went, eight fences in all. The in-and-out pointed toward the gate, and I just looked ahead at Jane, who was standing there, until just before the last fence, when I turned my head and stared beyond that one. As we approached the last fence, I stared at the barns, our goal, the place where we would go when this torture was over.

When we left through the gate, Jane said, "You got around. Not bad. A little slow, and he got that one rail with his back hoof, but a big improvement."

I hadn't even noticed the rail. That was good. That meant I was riding forward, not looking back.

I said, "I wasn't looking at the jumps, but he was. Every time we approach a fence, he starts shifting his weight backward and staring."

Jane said, "Hmm." But then there was the jump-off for the four horses who had gone clear. While Jane watched them, I led Blue back to his stall. He had done a lot today, and even here, by the coast, it was getting warm. I took off my hard hat, then untied my stock and patted my face with it.

One good thing about not having a groom is that you can talk to your horse while you are taking care of him. And so I talked to Blue. When I took off his saddle, I said, "Blue Blue, how are you?" He sniffed my hand for a bit of carrot. I scratched the top of his head and stroked his face. I took off the bridle and said, "There you go, much more comfortable." I put on the halter—he stuck his nose right into it. I cross-tied him. Then I pulled off my boots with the boot jack, not without saying to Blue, "Is it the boots that are bad luck?" I put on my old rubber boots, then I snapped the lead rope to the ring of his halter, took him off the cross-ties, picked up the scraper, and walked him over to the hose and hosed him all over. I scraped him down—he acted like I was tickling him, but politely. I said, "You're a good boy. There you go. I have two flakes of hay left, and you must be hungry." Blue shook his head when I gently hosed his face. Back at the stalls, I put him away, then found his lightest sheet and put it on him. I refilled his water bucket. I had never known a horse who felt as much like a friend as Blue.

Now I was on my own. I had three dollars in my pocket; it was lunchtime; I was finished showing. It was a wonderful feeling.

If you have school all day and horses to ride in the afternoon and on Saturday, homework in the evenings, family dinner, and church all day on Sunday, basically your time to yourself is while you are asleep. And my dad is always worried that time is being wasted. There is plenty to do on a ranch, even a small ranch like ours, and if you are sitting around, then maybe you should be cleaning tack. He doesn't even like me to read books while not doing anything. He says, "You could prop it up over the sink and read it while you're washing the dishes." I could. But here I was, no homework, no horsework, and no housework, wandering around the show grounds, knowing that my horse was happy eating his hay and I was free—I could do one thing at a time.

For that reason, I didn't find Jane. I watched the jumpers in the main ring while eating my hot dog, and I sat quietly with my lemonade, drinking it and then sucking on the lemon wedge. It was a jumper class, not terribly high—3'9", but that would be high to me now. The thing about jumping is that the jumps grow and shrink depending on how dependable your horse is. Black George—Onyx—had taken me over the giant ditch in the outside course, which was fifteen feet across, and it had felt simultaneously like flying and like no big deal. But that was Onyx. I had really enjoyed that horse, but there was a moment when I knew that I was just another human to him. I was training here at the stables, and the jumps got over four feet, and I lost my nerve. I dismounted and Sophia got on, and as they went into the ring, Black George didn't look back even once. I always had the feeling that Blue and Jack would have looked back, though I never said anything about that to Daddy, who was carrot-and-stick all the way, or Jane, who would surely tell me I was being sentimental.

And here was Sophia—speak of the devil. She was on the chestnut and they went around the course fairly smoothly. The only thing I saw that was wrong was that every so often he shook his head as if he was mad about something. Sophia was scowling when she left the ring, even though they had a clean round and were within the time. Then that boy Andy came in on the Appaloosa. The Appy was a nice type—bay with a white blanket over his haunches and spots on both hips, and a black tail. He didn't look like the other horses standing around—he was much flashier. The announcer said, "Now we have number three forty-five, Rascal, with Andrew Carmichael in the saddle."

Andy looked like he had all the time in the world. First they walked, then he shortened his reins, looked around, smiled, and picked up a trot. He settled in his saddle, and Rascal began to canter. It was a don't-mind-if-I-do sort of canter, easy as you please, and Andy looked like he was enjoying himself completely, not nervous in any way. They cantered down over the first coop, then turned back toward the second jump, an oxer, and looped around toward a line of three jumps, an in-and-out and then a brush. Rascal folded his legs neatly, but he was pretty flat over the fences, as if he didn't have to do much to accomplish his task. The last four jumps were a vertical, another oxer, another brush, and a gate. Rascal jumped all of them nicely and, you could say, exactly the same no matter what they were. The two of them came down to the trot just the way they had done everything else, easy as you please. And they, too, were within the time. When they left the ring, Daphne met him. They walked to the center of the warm-up, and Andy did a funny thing—he pushed himself backward off the saddle and slid down over Rascal's tail. Rascal didn't flick an ear. I laughed.

After the jump-off, Andy was fourth and Sophia was fifth. I thought that surely Andy should get the prize for having the most fun of anyone in the class. When he was around, everyone else looked too serious and worried by comparison. I watched the three of them, Andy, Daphne, and Rascal, walk back toward the barns.

By the time I had watched the 3'3" hunters, I was almost dozing off, and then I remembered the tack tent. The tack tent was where they sold all sorts of things for horses and riders—boots and breeches and saddles and bridles, brushes, blankets, shirts, saddle soap, belts with horseshoe buckles, hairnets, leather halters and brass nameplates, horse bandages, and also books about riding. That's what I thought I would go look at. Blue needed that, maybe. I got up and threw away my paper plate and my lemonade cup.

The weather was now perfect—the pine trees around the show grounds were brilliant green in the sunshine, and their tops were swaying slightly with the ocean breezes. The air was fresh and smelled of all sorts of things—pine needles, horse manure, the ocean, some sort of sweet flower (Mom would have known but I didn't). It was Thursday afternoon, and more horses were arriving for the weekend—glossy bays and chestnuts, a few grays and blacks. Not a single buckskin. We had had a buckskin, Daddy's favorite horse ever, Lester, but he'd sold him, just like he sold them all.

The tack tent was not far from the barns, so I checked on Blue. He was working on his hay. He looked up, nickered once, and went back to it. I said, "Good boy."

I knew that the saddles and bridles and boots and breeches

in the tack tent were none of my business, though I did let my hand run across the saddles just a bit.

The books were in the back, on a table. There were only about ten of them, and three of them were stories, not how-to books. I picked up the next one, which was called *The Cavalry Manual of Horsemanship and Horsemastership*. It was the official manual of the United States Cavalry School at Fort Riley. Colonel Hawkins, Jane's boss, who ran the barn, had gone to that cavalry school. It was in Kansas somewhere, which is right above Oklahoma, where my grandparents live. The front cover had a pretty drawing of a horse's head at the top. I saw that it was illustrated by an artist named Sam Savitt. I had never heard of him—the books I had at home were illustrated by someone named C. W. Anderson.

All the drawings in the book were of soldiers on horseback—they were wearing billed caps and light-colored jackets and ties, and they were sitting up as straight as could be. They were also all riding Blue, only as a bay or a chestnut, it looked like (they were pencil drawings, so they had no color). It really was strange to look at the pictures, especially the one that illustrated how you were supposed to sit—the horse had large eyes, forward ears, graceful neck, head a bit long but slender. Blue's spitting image. I, of course turned to the section about jumping, and then to the section about refusing, running out, and rushing. It wasn't very long. Right at the beginning, it read, "In order to stop at a jump, if he is going along at a good pace, he must lower his head." That seemed true, though I had thought Blue was lowering his head because he was staring at the jump, not to get away from my hands.

The next words were in italics, so I knew they were important: *"Therefore with a refuser, contact must never be lost."* Okay, I thought. "It is, however, very necessary that the hands follow the mouth while maintaining the heavier contact." I opened the front cover of the book and looked at the price. Five dollars. I had a dollar. I went back to reading. The part I didn't like, on the next page, was about punishing the refuser. "The moment after a refusal occurs, the offender should be faced squarely up against the center of the obstacle and punished sharply, just in the rear of the cinch, with the spurs or on the croup with the riding whip." I had not punished Blue after his refusal; I had just turned him around and headed him back over the fence, and he had jumped it. I couldn't imagine jabbing Blue with spurs (I didn't even wear spurs with him) or smacking him hard with the whip, but maybe I was going to have to do that.

Then I read about running out, which was a type of refusing where, instead of stopping, the horse ducks to one side, left or right. According to the book, whichever side your horse ducked toward, you would never turn that way—you would always turn him back the way he didn't want to go. While you were doing this, you were supposed to punish him with the spur on the same side you were turning toward. So let's say Blue and I were cantering down toward a brush fence and veered to the right. I would turn him back to the left and punish him behind the girth with the left spur. If I had a left spur. I was glad that Blue did not run out, at least so far.

The rushers were the scary ones. These were horses whose riders held them too tight as they went toward the fence, so the horse sped up and pushed forward in an attempt to get over the fence. Apparently, the worst thing you could do to a horse was hold him tight and kick him on, because he would get a little frantic. Then if you let go of his mouth over the fence, he would (or could) fall forward. If he was used to this, then in order not to fall, he would go faster. Even the thought of this made me nervous. I read, "To jump a rushing star-gazer is a dangerous ordeal. If he is rated, he cannot always see the jump, and if turned loose too late, a calamity is always imminent." I guessed that "rated" meant held too tight. I slammed the book shut and thought of my list of rules. The fact was that jumping was fun, but it was also a lot harder than I had thought it was. What in the world was I doing, teaching Melinda and Ellen? Well, this was what—I was relying on Gallant Man always to be a good boy. I set the book down. I touched the one beside it, called *Schooling Your Horse,* but to be honest, I was afraid to pick it up and open it. Then I saw the lady who ran the tack tent looking at me, and I realized that maybe I wasn't supposed to read the books without buying them. I stacked them the way I had found them, and wandered out of the tent. Danny would get there in about an hour. I didn't feel as happy as I had before I'd read that book.

When the clock said almost four, I made my way back to Blue's stall. He had finished the hay and was just standing there, resting. He stood up straight and nickered when he saw me. I still hadn't run into Jane, but maybe she had been looking for me, because there was a note in her handwriting, pinned to Blue's stall. It said, "For Tuesday. See you then. Call me if you need to," and underneath that, a typed sheet that

49

said, "Peter Finneran Clinic, 9:00 a.m. Tuesday, August 9, 1966. Horse: True Blue. Rider: Abby Lovitt. Morning clinic will last ninety minutes. Please dress in high boots, canary breeches, formal shirt, hard hat, gloves. No coats necessary. In the event of foul weather, the clinic will proceed. Please bring raincoat and crewneck sweater. Be prepared to jump; however, Tuesday's clinic will concentrate on flat work."

I pulled out the thumbtack, wrapped the tack in Jane's note, and carefully put it in my pocket. You do not ever want a thumbtack lying around where horses might walk—it could go right up into the sole of a horse's hoof. Then I found the bandages and went in to wrap Blue's legs for the trip home. Danny showed up when I was starting on the fourth one, the right hind. He said, "Hey. I'll take this stuff out." There wasn't much. Once I had finished with Blue and opened the stall door, all we had to do was load him into the trailer, close it up, and leave. By now it was a really beautiful day, so probably at home it was ninety-five. Whatever it was, Mom or Dad would be sure to tell me.

Blue, of course, loaded right on, and Danny closed his window while I closed the back door and latched it. Then we got into the truck. Danny was still wearing his swimming trunks, though with a regular shirt and his cowboy boots. He looked sort of weird, but I didn't say anything. His jeans were folded up on the floor by my feet and his hair was a mess. I guessed he had gone swimming, probably more than once. I had never gone swimming in the ocean. I could swim in a pool, but I would need a lot more practice to swim in the Pacific, which was cold anyway, and the thought of it did not make me want to try.

The radio was tuned to a rock-and-roll station, not Daddy's usual mumbly talking. When Danny turned on the engine, the Mamas and the Papas soared out of the speaker, singing "I Saw Her Again Last Night." That was a good song. Then the DJ spoke, then there was a weird one that I hadn't heard in a while, called "Eight Miles High," and then one about not bringing me down, which Danny sang along with as we drove through the pine forest. He even opened the window a little wider and sang it out the window. I was laughing.

As we were coming to the main road, a strange thing happened. This woman came on with a really good voice, and she was singing a song I had heard before, though I couldn't remember when, and Danny's eyes started to water. The song was something like "I Can't Help Falling in Love with You," and I wondered if Danny was thinking about Leah. It was a sad song, and after a little bit, I started feeling like crying myself. But we did not talk about it. It was a good thing that another loud song came on right after—"Yellow Submarine." When that came on, Danny turned it up even higher. I rode along with the wind in my face, and that was fun, too. When we were about a mile from our place, Danny turned the radio down, and then changed the station back to the mumbly talking. It was a good thing he did, because Daddy was standing right there when we pulled up to the gate.

Whip

Quirt

Chapter 4

SATURDAY NIGHT WAS THE PARTY. I WORE A GREEN COTTON skirt and a white shirt—very simple, as Mom said, but she gave me an old necklace she had, which was a silver heart and a silver violet hanging on a chain. I had some new pumps for school, black patent leather. They had one-and-a-half-inch heels. When I came downstairs to be driven to the party, Daddy wondered where my Mary Janes were, and before I could even answer, Mom said, "She outgrew those." Daddy looked surprised. Since I am now at least an inch taller than Mom, I think the reason for his surprise must be that he is so tall he can't tell the difference between us from way up there.

The Goldman twins had invited the whole eighth-grade class. We were about to be freshmen at the high school, so this was our last party with just us. I got there the same time as Larry Schnuck, who was wearing jeans, a T-shirt, and boots. The other boys had on regular button-downs, except for Billy Russell and Sergio Garcia, who were wearing cowboy shirts that my dad would have liked. The girls all looked less "simple" than I did—Linda A. had a tight skirt, black, which made me realize that green is a really boring color for a party. Alexis and Barbie had gone into their mother's and aunt's closets and come up with dresses from the 1940s. Alexis's was dark blue, with buttons down the front and short sleeves. The sleeves, the collar, and the pockets were trimmed with white, and she had found a pair of short white gloves. Barbie was wearing a shiny gray dress with a wide belt and a huge skirt, and under that was about ten acres of petticoat. She had on a small white hat pinned over her bun. They looked both fun and beautiful, and I missed them already. Barbie kissed me on the cheek and said she loved my necklace.

Stella and Gloria were very up to date. Gloria was wearing a nice sleeveless dress in beige and gray. The beige top came straight across and then angled down toward the waist, and then the gray skirt flared out. She looked right out of *Seventeen*. Stella had on windowpane hose, white culottes, and a short square jacket. She looked really good, and I saw the others watching her.

The first thing I did, though, was go into the kitchen and find the cat, Staccato. He had been our kitten, and we had given him to Barbie and Alexis. He was half grown now, tall and thin. When he saw me, he came over and rubbed against my legs, then he squatted down with his front and back paws neatly together and his tail wrapped around them. He closed his eyes and started purring, waiting for me to pet him, which I did. I said, "To think you could have ended up a mangy barn cat, running away from every human instead of being spoiled rotten." After a moment, he slumped to the side and stretched out, half opening his eyes, as if to say, "Mmmm. Spoiled rotten is good."

In the family room, Barbie and Alexis were dividing us into teams, one to be led by Barbie, of course, and one to be led by Alexis. We were going on a scavenger hunt. They had typed out a list for each team of the things we were supposed to find. We had an hour and a half—sunset was around eight. We could go anywhere in the neighborhood, including knocking on doors and asking for things, but the whole team had to be back by eight, or we would forfeit the game.

Kyle Gonzalez said, "What's the prize?"

Barbie said, "Status."

Kyle looked disappointed.

I was on Barbie's team. There were twenty-five items on the list. One was a single Cheerio. Another was a baby diaper. The weirdest one, I thought, was a recording by Frank Sinatra. The list read as follows:

> A postcard from somewhere east of California
> Last week's edition of *Time* magazine
> A roll of Life Savers
> A sprig of wild rosemary
> A single Cheerio
> A red rose

A left-hand glove
A baby diaper
A book from Reader's Digest Condensed Books
A can of tuna
An acorn
A partly filled-in crossword puzzle
A barrette
A safety pin
A green crayon
A toy car
A photograph of someone nobody knows
A pat of butter
Last Sunday's newspaper
A lug nut
A Coke bottle
A rubber band
A chopstick
A recording by Frank Sinatra
A hat

I wondered if Barbie and Alexis knew what a lug nut was.

Barbie said, "All the neighbors know us, and are never surprised by anything we do." In the last fifteen minutes, we could run back to the Goldmans' house and look for what we hadn't been able to find (but there was no guarantee that any of these things was there) or we could keep combing the neighborhood—we had to vote which one to do. Kyle and Stella were on our team, also Billy, Maria, and Lucia. Mrs. Goldman shouted, "One, two, three, go!" and we ran out of the house, following either Barbie or Alexis. Alexis turned right and Barbie turned left. Almost as soon as we got into the street, Kyle bent down and plucked something. It was the sprig of rosemary. Barbie put it into her paper bag. Maria said, "Can we produce something ourselves, or do we have to find it?"

Barbie looked at her a moment, then said, "We didn't talk about that, so either way."

Maria reached into her pocket and brought out a safety pin. Barbie smiled and dropped it into the bag. She said, "Only one minute gone."

It became my job to go to the nearest front door and ask for a Cheerio. The lady was nice—she waved to Barbie and smiled—but no Cheerios, only Rice Krispies. As we were crossing to the next house, Kyle picked up an acorn; I knew from my seventh-grade mission project that having Kyle on your team was always an advantage. The high school kid at the next house had a Cheerio. Kyle then asked him for a Kleenex, which he also had, and Kyle wrapped the Cheerio in the Kleenex and put it in his pocket.

And so we went along, asking for things and finding things. Billy and Martin Orlovsky seemed to think that trash cans were the key, and sure enough, they did find some things, including the red rose—wilted, but recognizable—and the *Time* magazine, last Sunday's newspaper, the Coke bottle, and, strangely enough, the hat—a torn straw hat, but nobody said things had to be new. Barbie would not let them look for the baby diaper in the trash—she herself asked for that at the Barkins' house, since they had a new baby. She promised to bring it back in the morning, and Mr. Barkin said, "Please, not too early." He did look tired.

It was Kyle who found the lug nut. We were walking along,

and only Kyle was looking down. As we passed one car, he said, "I see one." It was lying on the ground, between the car's tire and the curb. He bent down and picked it up.

Billy said, "Now that wheel's going to fall off."

Kyle said, "We didn't remove the lug nut. It was lying there. Anyway"—he looked at the tire—"it has few more."

Lucia said, "I think we should—"

"Leave a note," said Barbie. She tore a piece off the paper bag and wrote, "Your lug nut is at #246, up the street." She stuck it under the windshield wiper, and Kyle dropped the lug nut into the bag.

By 7:40, we had found everything except the Frank Sinatra recording, the toy car, and the chopstick. Barbie was not allowed by the rules to say whether those things were at her house, but it was getting cold, so I voted to go back there and take our chances—after all, we had the lug nut. I was in the majority, and we were pretty far from the house, so once we had voted, Barbie said, "Run!" and we ran. It was fun. We got warm, and we were laughing by the time we got there. Alexis and her group had decided to stay out. It wasn't quite dark, but almost. The house was bright—every room was lit up. While we were gone, Mrs. Goldman and her sister, Mrs. Marx, had put all kinds of food on the dining room table, and it made me hungry just to see it.

Barbie had to sit down and stay silent while we looked for our last three things. She couldn't even roll her head around to tell us where to go, or shout "Warm!" or "Cold!" Kyle went straight into the kitchen and started looking through all the drawers for a chopstick, but Stella found it in the pantry, in a picnic basket. The Frank Sinatra recording was not by the stereo in the living room, but upstairs, in Barbie and Alexis's room, right next to the Rolling Stones. It was the toy car that stumped us, and when the other kids ran in at two minutes to eight, we still hadn't found one.

It was completely dark when they got there, and as they came in, we could hear a couple of coyotes out in the valley howling and yipping. Everyone's hair was all wild and our clothes were messed up, but we were laughing like crazy. Barbie and Alexis poured out our finds on the coffee table, and Kyle set the Kleenex with the Cheerio in it on top of our things.

The other team did have a toy car and they also had a red rose, a fake—but nothing on the list said it had to be real. They did not have a lug nut. Other than those things, both teams had found everything on the list—Alexis, too, had stopped at the Birkins' house, and Mrs. Birkin had given her a diaper. It looked like there was going to be a tie, until it came to the pat of butter. Ours was wrapped in waxed paper; theirs had melted into the old newspaper. You could see a big oily circle, but no pat. Mrs. Goldman agreed that we won. Our reward was that we got to eat first, and we were hungry. There were hamburgers and hot dogs, potato chips and drop doughnuts. The closest they came to something strange was apple brown Betty, which was crunchy bread crumbs over cooked apples, like a pie but sweeter.

By the time I was finished eating, all the other girls had gone into the bathroom to comb their hair, put on more lipstick, and straighten their outfits. Stella had completely redone her French twist and I thought she looked really good. I couldn't figure out why Gloria kept looking at me and opening her eyes really wide and then closing them again, but then I looked more carefully at Stella and saw that she was wearing false eyelashes. I didn't know how I'd missed them—they went halfway up to her eyebrows. But she looked good anyway. Gloria didn't need to go into the bathroom. She could redo her lipstick and fix her hair by feel. She practiced it because it was "an essential skill," according to her. One wall of her room was a big bulletin board, and on it she tacked a Polaroid picture of herself that she took every morning before she went to school. Her mother just laughed and said it was an "art installation."

We danced. I didn't dance every time, or even most of the time, but the music just kept going, and pretty soon everyone who wanted to dance was dancing, girls with girls, girls with boys, boys with boys. Barbie and Alexis got me up out of a chair once and made me twirl around and around, both directions, until I was crying with laughter. Then we jumped up and down until we fell onto the couch. Everyone who did not want to dance sat around looking at the ones who did and yawning. It was an active party. There wasn't a single moment where you wondered, "What next?" except in a bigger way—once the Goldmans were gone, what was the next thing we were going to do for fun? I had no idea. When Mom came to pick me up at a quarter to eleven, Alexis hugged me at the door, and Barbie walked me to the car. She put something in my hand. It was a box of sugar cubes—brown ones—for Blue, the horse she liked to ride. She gave me two kisses on the cheek and said, "One of those is for him, okay?"

She stood and waved as we drove away.

Mom knew better than to ask me how I felt.

I spent Monday preparing for the clinic and trying not to think, Well, they must be heading to the airport now, well, they must be on the plane now. I cleaned and oiled my tack, ironed my shirt, and put some spot remover on a little stain on my canary breeches. I polished my boots. I found an old sweater of Mom's, a green crewneck from who knew when. The sleeves were too short, but I thought I could push them up if I had to put it on. My raincoat was not very good for riding, but it wasn't supposed to rain.

We gave Blue a bath and combed his mane. We put some oil in his tail to help us comb it out, and washed his white foot with extra soap, then wrapped the two front legs. He was going to stay in that night so he would still be clean in the morning. Unlike the others, he didn't mind, because he had his hay all to himself. By the end of the day, I felt almost normal—and rather proud of Blue.

A clinic, it turns out, is a lot like school. After nine years of school, including kindergarten, I won't say that I felt right at home, but I did feel as though I'd been there before. There were fourteen of us on our horses in the big arena at exactly 9:00 a.m. We were to ride together for the first session, then split up into three groups for the real jumping. Obviously, Blue and Onyx would not be jumping in the same group.

I saw Sophia and another girl from the stables named Alice, and a few whose names I didn't know but whom I had watched at shows. There were eight I had never seen before. Sophia, I knew, was fourteen already, and I would be fourteen in a few weeks. Everyone else looked like they were fifteen, sixteen, or seventeen. We were on all kinds of horses. There was a very flashy bald-faced bay with four white socks, and another bay, a mare, who didn't have a white hair on her but was so graceful that she looked flashy, too. Her name, I heard them say, was Parisienne. That part was like school, too—some horses were beautiful, some were smart, some were show-offy, and some kept to themselves, and one, a chestnut, looked mad about everything, and reminded me of Rally—Ornery George, whom we'd sold to a rancher and never heard about again (which is what happens most of the time). Blue was the only gray.

Peter Finneran had those bowlegs you see on lifelong horsemen like Daddy and Danny, except that his bowlegs were inside very elegant black boots. He was short—I guessed that if I were to stand up next to him, we would see eye to eye. His breeches were not canary, either—they were a sort of beigy sand color that made canary look "loud," as Mom would say. His shirt was blue and he had on a tweed wool cap with a snapped bill. The most unusual thing about him was the way he walked. He didn't roll a bit from side to side, like Daddy and Danny; he seemed to spring from here to there, like he just couldn't contain himself. And for such a small guy, he had a very loud voice.

"Ah," he said, "California girls! Hair everywhere, shirts not tucked in, leathers out of their keepers, dirty horses." He walked over to one of the chestnuts and flicked something off the horse's shoulder. "I can tell you girls have never served in the U.S. Army." Two of the girls looked at each other sort of nervously, as though they were wondering if they'd missed an assignment—the assignment of serving in the U.S. Army. Then he said, "You know, young ladies, just because you haven't been told to do something, that doesn't mean you just sit there slouching in your saddles, letting your horses do whatever they please." He looked straight at that same chestnut, who was tossing his head like he had a fly on his nose. "Stand up now! Form a line along here, right in front of me. It should be in order of size, but my guess is that's beyond you."

We lined up the way you do after a hack class in a show. I put Blue between Parisienne and one of the chestnuts. Onyx was at the far end. Sophia did not have her hair everywhere, because she wore braids, and thanks to Rodney, no leathers were out of their keepers. Peter Finneran walked down the line, stopping at each horse and asking for the rider's name, the horse's name, and where they were from. Then he would say the names and ask a question or two. He started with Sophia, but I couldn't hear him very well until he got to Parisienne.

"Name?"

"Nancy Howard."

"Nancy." He made her name sound like a bit of a joke. "Horse?"

"Parisienne."

"Parisienne. You are from?"

"Here."

He laughed. "Show experience?"

"Parisienne was a first-year green hunter last year, champion at four shows. Then I got her. This year, she's gone second-year green and gotten some ribbons at two shows—"

"Going into decline, then?"

Nancy looked a little shocked at this, and began to say, "Well, I—"

"Does your opinion matter? I'm giving the clinic. It's my opinion that matters. We will figure it out. What is she, an old racehorse?"

"She was bred for the track, but I don't think she ran."

"Well, that's good and that's bad. It's good, because she's probably pretty sound, but it's bad, because they had some reason to reject her."

In the midst of Nancy's shrug of ignorance, Peter Finneran turned suddenly to me and said, "Name?"

"Abby Lovitt."

"Abby. Horse?"

"True Blue."

"True Blue. How sentimental. I recognize him. Pretty worthless in the show, wasn't he?"

I didn't speak or move.

"Ah. Struck dumb. Where are you from?"

I had to clear my throat. "We have a ranch in the valley."

"Experience?"

"I usually ride western. We just got Blue in the spring. That was his first show."

"I could tell." He was already looking at the chestnut, though, and then he went on. Nancy and I exchanged a glance that said, Well, that's over anyway.

Once he had come to the end of the line and recited our names in a list, he sent us to the rail and watched us for a long time, it seemed, and it felt like a test. You went around and went around, and the longer you walked and then trotted, the more self-conscious you got. Who was he looking at? Thank goodness, not me.

And yet the ninety minutes passed pretty quickly. With fourteen horses in the ring, he didn't have much to say to any one person. His comments were not about heels down or look ahead or chin up, like a riding lesson. They were about "I need to see some energy in that mare, Margie. Sit deeper and push her on with your legs," or "Square corners, Eileen. Your horse is able to bend, even if you don't realize it." Blue's flat work was good, and I made sure to ask him to lift his inside shoulder the way Jem Jarrow taught. I even sort of lost track of where I was during the canter, because Blue's canter was so dreamy and light. I got a compliment when we had to do the voltes, which were small circles. Blue and I started ours just where we were told to, and made just the right size circle, perfectly round. Peter Finneran boomed out, "See that, girls? Very precise. If she can do it, you can do it."

The important thing, I came to realize, was following instructions exactly. When he said, "Canter at the light pole," your horse had to go into the canter as your leg was passing the light pole. When he said, "Rein back four steps," you had to know how to count to four, not five. It was surprising how hard this exercise was. When he asked for a figure eight, first at the trot and then at the canter, you had to make circles and change direction right in the middle. Thanks to Danny, Blue could do this, with a flying change of lead in both directions. I did not get a compliment, but I didn't get what Nancy got, either. Parisienne changed only her front legs, not her back legs, for the flying change, and went on like that for four strides without Nancy realizing it. Peter Finneran exclaimed, "Nancy! Is there a brain in that blond head? Oh, these California girls!"

Yes, I was lulled. After exactly fifty minutes, we lined up at one end of the arena, and Rodney and another groom set up some cavalletti—four in a row. One by one, we trotted down over these. Onyx went first, which was probably bad for the rest of us, because he sparkled through, springing his body and lifting his legs. I could see that he was thinking, At last the jumps! Everyone after him looked a little clumsier and not as attentive. Blue knocked the first one with his hoof, but then got the others right. Peter Finneran exclaimed, "You girls know how they did this at Fort Riley? Nose to tail! If you did that, these horses would fall over. Pick it up, ladies!" We tried again. After four times, everyone was fine. Peter Finneran was staring at Onyx and Sophia. I was sure he thought they were the best.

Now Rodney and the other groom came out and removed the cavalletti, then set up two small jumps in the center of the arena, end to end, sort of the way they would be in the warm-up at a show. Both were simple verticals. Then they put poles in front of each of them—for one, there were two poles on the barn side, and for the other, there were two poles on the woods side. We were to trot down over the poles and jump the first fence, then turn and canter the poles and jump the second fence. The fences were about 2'9". Without me trying to re-member, I thought of those pictures in the cavalry manual, of the horse who looked just like Blue cantering down to the fence, jumping it, and cantering away. I made myself get straight like the soldier in the picture—lifting my hands a little bit, pushing my heels down, tucking my chin. When it came to my turn, I picked up the trot and headed for the first jump. After three strides, I was the soldier in the picture.

Unfortunately, Blue was not the horse in the picture. He trotted the poles, but stared at the vertical, then hesitated for just a moment and finally popped over. I went on, but I was really embarrassed—I could feel that my face was red. When we made the loop, Blue tossed his head and picked up the wrong lead. I had to stop him and start again, which made me feel even more awkward. Then he half stumbled over the canter poles, and hesitated again before the jump. He did jump it, though. I glanced at Peter Finneran. He was shaking his head.

But there were other horses, and we had to finish the class. For the next twenty minutes, each of the horses did the same exercise. We all did it three times altogether. I can't say that Blue was perfect or even good, but he did get better each time. At exactly 10:30, Peter Finneran lined us up and dismissed us. We would get our group assignments after lunch.

The afternoon class, which only lasted forty-five minutes, was pretty much fun. There were four of us in it—not Sophia and not Nancy, just me and three other girls on young horses (a four-year-old and a couple of five-year-olds). One of them was something called a "cob," from England, which was wide and wooly like a pony, but a normal horse size. The girl who was riding him, Lucy, had an English accent. She was down from Woodside and was training the horse, Donegal, for the hunt field. Peter Finneran seemed to like him. He said he was "old-fashioned and unpretentious."

Our exercises were much simpler, all over poles on the ground. Rodney and the other groom set up the poles to look like jumping courses, but they were only poles, so we trotted and cantered and galloped over them, made our turns, and practiced our lead changes and trot diagonals without being nervous about the jumps. The biggest jump we had was two poles next to one another. I have to say that Blue noticed the two poles, and made a little bigger jump than he did with one pole. I wanted Peter Finneran to see this and to say something nice about how observant Blue was, but he just nodded and turned to the next horse. However, I enjoyed myself (mostly because we got to canter a lot) and by the end of the day, I felt pretty good. Not everybody did. One girl in our class, who was riding a tidy little chestnut, the four-year-old, started crying as we walked back to the barns, and I heard Lucy say to her, "Now, don't be at that, Monica. He can hear you, and it just makes him worse."

Monica said, "Who does he think he is?"

Lucy said, "He thinks he's an Olympic horseman, and he is."

"She's four years old."

"Well, maybe you shouldn't have brought her, then, if she's not ready."

Monica sniffled a few more times but didn't say anything. At the barns, they were stabled pretty far away from me, so we didn't talk. I untacked Blue and brushed him down, then gave him a couple of carrots and his hay and water and put his sheet on him. Rodney was supposed to look in on him at the evening feeding time. When Mom picked me up and asked me about the clinic, I said it was fine. *Fine* is a good word, because you are not actually lying and saying that it was fun or good or enjoyable. You might just be saying that you could stand it. Mom didn't press me. Since Daddy was coming to watch the next day, I guess she thought she would find out then.

When we got home, it was only three thirty, so I changed into jeans and cowboy boots and took Oh My for a walk down to the crick. It was totally relaxing, and I was reminded how nice it is to ride a horse out for a walk. Rusty came along with us, and I'm sure Rusty had business of some sort, since she kept racing away and then circling back, and looking up into the trees and off toward the horizon. Rusty always felt she had two jobs, one of which was to protect the ranch and the other of which was to keep her eye on Mom in case Mom wanted to pet her. Oh My was a little like Rusty in the sense that she enjoyed getting out and having a look at things. She was one of the few horses I've known who wanted to investigate. For example, let's say you were passing a stump among the trees. Oh My would look at the stump, then she would go over to the stump and stand there sniffing the stump for a while. Every time you passed the stump after that, she would glance at it to see, I suppose, if it was the same as it had been the time before. Daddy said that this was a sign of intelligence, and it was no surprise that Oh My had made herself the boss of the mare band in the space of about five minutes when we turned her out in the pasture. After I came back with Oh My, I put Jack in the pen and worked him for twenty minutes. He could do all sorts of things, now—walk, trot, canter in both directions for however long you wanted, come, pivot both directions, back up, touch his nose to his side. I had also taught him a trick that I'd taught Blue—to see a treat, but then to turn his head away in order to get it. I'd taught Blue a second trick, which I called "Where's the carrot?" I would do what grown-ups used to do when we were kids, show him the bit of carrot in one hand, then pass it back and forth and put my hands behind my back. Then I would say, "Where's the carrot?" and Blue would nudge my right arm and I would give him the carrot. That was because the carrot was always in my right hand, but I played it up by pretending he had picked the proper arm. I hadn't taught Jack that trick yet. Daddy said not to teach them tricks like bowing or rearing, because you could be trotting along out there, give a mistaken command, and suddenly he'd bow.

I put Jack in with the others and got the wheelbarrow and the hay. Of course, I still had to clean my boots and iron my other shirt. By bedtime, I was actually looking forward to the next day. I'd decided that maybe Peter Finneran hadn't been that bad. The horses, including Blue, had improved, and the exercises had been fun.

Since we were the lowest-level group, we were to be on our horses and lined up by nine, but then we would be out of there by ten thirty, so Mom was planning to take me clothes shopping for the school year—high school would be starting one week after the clinic. I had spent the entire summer not thinking about high school, even though that was all that Gloria and Stella talked about. Gloria had already bought all of her new clothes, and had shown them to me the last time I spent the night at her house. Gloria had grown, too, and now she was about a quarter inch taller than I was, and "developed," as her mom said. She had worn the same shoe size for a year, so she was "done" and her mom decided to splurge on some "classics" for Gloria. I thought they seemed a little fancy for high school, but I had no idea, really. She had also gotten her hair cut in what she called a "five-point" style. It was short and thick, and it came down over the forehead and in front of her ears, and then in a point at the middle of her neck in back. She had to get up and style it every morning, but that was like her hobby, and she didn't mind. Stella I hadn't seen except at the Goldmans' party. Gloria said that Stella was planning on wearing her French twist every day. I didn't really have a hair plan for high school, which made me a little nervous. Anyway, because Mom was taking me to the department store, she decided to stay and watch the clinic.

We lined our horses up at the end of the arena, because four jumps had been built in the middle in an X. Two arms of the X were verticals—the east arm and the north arm; the west arm was an oxer, and the south arm was a brush.

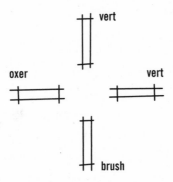

There were poles in front of the verticals, but not in front of the oxer or the brush. Blue did very nice flat work—precise and energetic—so Peter Finneran actually said, "Abby, you or someone has done a good job with this horse." I didn't answer, but I smiled the way you are supposed to when you get a compliment. The same could not be said for Monica. At one point in the flat work, her mare grabbed the bit, tossed her head, and started bucking. Peter Finneran began shouting, "Kick her on, Monica! Make her go forward! Doesn't she know the most basic things? Don't you?" Penny and her five-year-old brown gelding always got the same response: "Okay. That will do." He continued to like Donegal—at least he would smile when Donegal was slow in his responses, and say, "Well, he's a bit thick, but he's doing his best." Lucy scowled, which indicated to me that "a bit thick" wasn't a compliment. However, when the jumping started, Donegal went first and he just galloped down over the fences, not looking right or left. I guess that was why Peter Finneran liked him.

Our job over the fences started easy and got hard. First we were to trot and canter over the smaller vertical, then to canter that same vertical, turn right, make a loop, and canter the larger vertical. Then we were to do these two, canter out, come back over the brush, turn right again, and canter down over the oxer. I saw that by the end of the lesson, we would probably be approaching each of these fences from both sides, making a course of eight jumps with lots of turns and loops. Really, it was like the day before with the poles. The jumps themselves were not terribly hard, and the turns were not tight. The "courses" Peter Finneran made of these four jumps were smoother and less complicated than show courses, and there was a part of me that really liked the idea. There was not a part of Blue that really liked the idea. All of the other horses were better than he was, even the four-year-old. After the first two-jump section, for which Blue was his nervous self, Peter Finneran handed me a whip. When I took it by the handle with the lash pointing down, he took it back and turned it so the lash pointed upward. Then he said, "This is a whip. If your horse doesn't go willingly to the jump, then you must actually use this implement to remind him of his job. With this animal, I think once will be enough, but you have to mean it."

I said, "To mean what?" But I knew what he wanted me to do. He wanted me to take my reins in my left hand and smack Blue a good one on the haunches as soon as he shifted his weight backward or showed hesitation. Daddy would have certainly agreed, but he would have used a quirt, not a whip. That was what the expression "the carrot or the stick" was all about. If a horse didn't understand something, then you made him understand it, either by showing him some food or giving him some pain. The problem was that I had decided in the spring, when we first got Blue, that he liked the carrot and hated the stick. I had never whipped him because I thought it would just make him more nervous. I looked Peter Finneran in the eye, and I almost said, "He won't like it," but thinking about what he had said to the other girls, and the fact that his mind was not going to be changed by a thirteen-year-old, I nodded. Holding the whip as he had shown me, I turned Blue away from him, picked up the trot, then the canter, and went down to the jump. When Blue pricked his ears and hesitated three strides out, I brought the whip down on his right haunch, and a moment later over he went, high and fast.

Peter Finneran waved me over to him. He said, "Now, you

do the exercises, and you make sure you carry that whip the way I showed you, so that he can see it. He's felt it once. Maybe he'll need to feel it again, but maybe not. But he does need to see it." He stared at me until I nodded.

After that we did all our jumping exercises the way we were told to do—over, turn, back, over, out and around, over, turn the other way, back, out and around. Over. Every time fast and high. When ten thirty rolled around, I was a little surprised. I was also breathing hard, and Blue was sweating and panting. Donegal, by contrast, was cool and dry.

I saw Mom from time to time as I went around. She met me when we came out of the gate and walked with me back to the barns. She held Blue while I hosed him off, and she put his sheet on him. She gave him two carrots and fluffed up the straw in his stall. But she didn't say a word. And when we went shopping, she let me pick my own clothes—two sweaters and two skirts, a jacket, a pair of brown loafers, and two shirts. I also tried on this A-line black-and-white geometric dress with short sleeves and a square neckline. We both really liked it, but it cost forty dollars and we could not imagine where in the world I would wear it.

When we got back to the stables in the afternoon to check on Blue and give him his hay and water for the night, Jane came running up to us and said, "Peter Finneran has told me, Abby, that he would like you to ride a more experienced horse tomorrow. Sophia and her dad have agreed to let you ride Pie in the Sky."

"That's the chestnut?"

Jane nodded, then said, "You'll do fine on him, Abby. He's been waiting for someone like you, to tell the truth."

I didn't know if that was a good thing.

She must have read my expression, because she said, "Come out early and ride him for a bit. Sophia won't be here until the afternoon, and if you're going to ride him for Peter Finneran, you need to get used to him."

I said, "What time?"

"Eight would be good."

I saw what she meant. Colonel Hawkins would not be around at eight.

Announcer's Stand

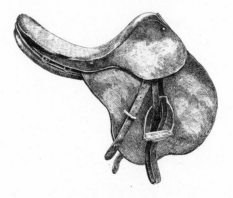

Pariani Saddle

Chapter 5

When I first saw her, Sophia had two horses, a gray mare and Pie in the Sky. The gray mare won a lot, but she was a hunter, and after getting Onyx, Sophia had decided that riding jumpers was more interesting. Also, as Jane had told me, "they got a nice piece of change" for the gray mare, who ended up down in Los Angeles. Sophia didn't seem to like Pie in the Sky, but he had won a few classes, including, Jane said, an important one at the recent show. I had seen Pie in the Sky jump several impressive courses, but I had also seen him refuse. Once he refused so sharply that Sophia slipped forward and had to grab his neck not to fall off. This did not make me want to ride him, so that night I called Danny.

He sounded kind of sleepy when he answered, but I ignored

that and said, "Can you come to the stables and help me with Pie in the Sky?"

"Who's Pie in the Sky?"

"He belongs to that girl, Sophia, who bought Black George. He's her other jumper. I'm supposed to ride him in the clinic."

"Why?"

"Because they want me to jump big jumps, I guess."

"I gotta work."

"Can you please call Jake and ask if you can get there at nine thirty or something? I am a little scared of him. He's tricky." Then I thought of something. "He cost them fifteen thousand dollars."

"He did?"

I said, "Mmmp," which I knew Danny would think was a yes. I was sure Danny would be very interested in a fifteen-thousand-dollar horse. Of course, I had no idea how much Pie in the Sky had cost, but I also thought that Sophia wouldn't look at a cheap horse, or even a rather expensive horse. Only a *very* expensive horse would be allowed to hang around if Sophia didn't like him.

He said, "Okay. Forty-five minutes. I'll pick you up and we'll drive out there and you'll have exactly forty-five minutes of my precious time."

Well, it was precious, at least where horses were concerned.

Jane, of course, had told Rodney when we would be there, and Pie in the Sky was tacked up and ready, with his own Pariani saddle, running martingale, breastplate, and jumping boots. He looked like he was about to go into battle. Rodney seemed to know perfectly well what we were doing there—he pointed to one of the far-off smaller rings and said, "Well, miss, I'm guessing you'll have that spot all to yourselves."

I said, "Thanks, Rodney."

He said, "Watch yerself, then, miss." Rodney had never cautioned me before. He and Danny exchanged a glance.

But I don't know if there was a horse that had ever made Danny nervous—and it wasn't just because he would ride anything. It was because he wasn't too lazy to take his time and be careful. In this case, as soon as we got to that small arena, with Pie in the Sky snorting all the way, he took all that tack off the horse and let him skitter around on his own for five minutes. Then he stepped forward and began to direct the skittering, so that Pie in the Sky could still be moving, but he had to move because Danny told him to, and in the direction Danny indicated. In another five minutes, Pie in the Sky was no longer skittering—he was trotting around and then cantering around, smooth, though fast, with big strides, and with his neck arched and his ears forward. Danny stepped over to him, put the bridle back on, and asked him to step under. He didn't know what we were talking about, but he was willing. I saw that he was pretty supple, either from training or naturally; stepping under was something he could easily do.

Then Danny put the saddle back on him with the breastplate, but not the running martingale, and let him do all his moves with that darn stuff flapping all over him. He settled down. And then he did a funny thing. He turned, dropped his head, and came over to us. His face was calm and he was not looking for carrots. I petted Pie in the Sky on his bright red cheek and said, "What's this all about?"

"I think he's saying he's ready. It's not like he doesn't know what his job is."

Danny stroked him down his neck, tightened the girth, and then cupped his hands. I went over and he legged me up into the saddle. Danny said, "Step him over a few times, both directions."

This was the great Jem Jarrow lesson for all horses and riders—you lift the horse's head to one side with the rein, and he learns to soften his back and step one hind leg across in front of the other, thereby turning his body in a small circle. It shows him where his feet are (you would be surprised how many horses have no idea where their feet are), it loosens his muscles, and it also makes him aware of the rider as someone who does something other than kicking him forward or pulling him back (or both at once). After we did this a few times, I trotted him in curving lines around the arena, asking him to change direction over and over. He did it, as I would expect him to.

It wasn't that he had no bad habits—he stuck his nose out more than I liked, and his idea whenever he didn't understand something was to go fast. But he felt agile and mostly willing. By the time Danny had to leave to get to work, I was as comfortable on Pie in the Sky as I was on most horses that I rode for the first time—there is always the first time. No horse feels the same as any other horse.

I took Pie in the Sky back to Rodney, and Rodney gave me a pat on the shoulder and said, "Yer a quiet thing, miss, but tough as an old boot, aren't ya?" I did not know if this was a compliment.

I went over to the big arena, where Lucy, Monica, and Penny had been joined by Nancy on Parisienne. It was after nine, so they were already going at it. Peter Finneran had his back to me, his hands on his hips. The girls were doing flat work—they were walking. But even so, Peter Finneran had plenty to say. "What do you girls think a walk is? A stroll? No sirree! A walk is a four-beat gait, four distinct beats. That horse needs to be saying, 'I am walking, hut two three four, hut two three four.' That horse needs to soften his jaw and hinge at the poll and step out step out step out. And he needs to go straight. Lucy! Your horse is going sideways, and you don't even know it, do you? Where is your hind end? Your horse's hind end? Well, it is not behind you, it's beside you! It's going to pass you if you don't watch out. Come over here!"

Lucy and Donegal turned and walked over to Peter Finneran. They halted in front of him, and he said, "Here's a funny thing that is especially obvious on this horse. His back end is wider than his front end. It's true of every horse, even the most delicate Thoroughbred!" He nodded toward Parisienne. "No, keep walking! You can do two things at once, I hope!" With two little motions, he made Donegal stand square, then he said, "If you are moving straight forward and your horse's spine is straight, then he cannot be parallel to the rail. There are sometimes when I want him to be parallel to the rail—so that he is a tiny bit bent to the outside—but I want you to know the difference between parallel to the rail and

81

therefore a little bent, and straight, therefore not parallel to the rail. Lucy, sit up, apply your legs equally, and look ahead." She walked a few strides, and Donegal looked straight to me. He did have large haunches, and you could see that he was a little triangular from front to back. Peter Finneran said, "When do you want them absolutely straight?"

Nobody dared answer. All of a sudden, he whipped around and said, "Abby? What do you think?"

I said, "Going down to a jump?"

"Finally! Some sense! Yes. Now, I want you girls to turn your horses in a line and walk down the center of the arena and see if you can sit up, go straight, and balance these animals."

I backed away from the arena, and carried the sack Mom had given me of peanut butter and jam sandwiches for breakfast around the big announcer's stand and clock stand to where Peter Finneran couldn't see me and I couldn't see him. But I could hear him. It was exhausting. The clock said nine thirty. My group didn't go until after lunch.

The morning was very dull except for one time when Jane came out of her office, saw me, and said, "Oh, come talk to me for five minutes. I feel like I've hardly seen you lately."

The stables hadn't stopped for Peter Finneran. He had the big arena, but other lessons were being given, trail rides were going out, and the grooms and workers were cleaning stalls, turning out horses, and otherwise tending to the stable business.

Jane had papers laid out on her desk—a map of the stables with names written over each stall. She also had a pad of paper and a stack of envelopes. I thought maybe she was making up bills or something like that. I sat down.

She went around, plopped into her desk chair, and said, "You know how to make sure you never ride?"

I shook my head.

"Run a stable!" She laughed. Then she leaned forward and said, "Did you ride Pie in the Sky?"

I nodded. "Danny helped me."

"He's not a bad horse. He's got air to spare."

"What does that mean?"

"I saw him jump a five-foot course one day, easy as you please. He's got amazing spring. But they—well, anyway. I'm sure your brother had a few ideas."

"Pie in the Sky came right over to us when he was finished loosening up, like he was saying he was ready."

"They do lunge him. But he's so valuable that they never let him play or jump around. Might hurt himself. Not my business, but it could be said that if Sophia would pay more attention to him, she might like him better." Then she looked at me and said, "When you're going down to the jump, sit up a little. That's all. I'll be finished with this in time to come watch you."

The first thing I did when we were mounted and doing our own flat work was lift the inside rein every so often, at the walk, trot, and canter, and in both directions—not enough for Peter Finneran to see, but enough for Pie in the Sky to feel and to respond to by lifting his inside shoulder and relaxing his back. When Jem Jarrow first taught me that trick, it had worked even with Rally—or Ornery George, as he was called then—who was about as stiff in his back as a horse could be.

We did half an hour of flat work, and I could see Sophia watching me, and Sophia could see me watching her. The best thing for getting used to another person riding your horse (and there was still a part of me that thought of Onyx as my horse) is to watch that person riding your horse—after a while, he stops looking like your horse, and she stops looking so odd on him. Sophia was maybe the thinnest person I ever saw, but not skinny—more like made of steel cables. She had long braids to the middle of her back, thick and blond, and she had big braces in a thin face. As far as I could tell, Black George behaved perfectly for her. But Peter Finneran acted and talked like he thought she was a mess. If he wasn't shouting, "Corner, Sophia!" then he was shouting, "Sophia! Please ask that horse to wake up!" or "Elbows, Sophia! Bend your elbows!" And then once we were warmed up, instead of having us trot over a jump (there were six set up, plus a long row of crossbars), he had us line up and dismount. Then, one by one, he got on each of our horses and took him or her down over a vertical, maybe 3'3", and four strides after that, a triple bar, a pretty high jump, maybe 3'6". The first one he got on was Onyx. Once he was mounted, he said to us, "All right. I'm going to jump the first jump the way you girls jump, and then I'm going to jump the second jump the way it should be done."

He turned Onyx in a small circle and cantered toward the first jump. At the very last moment, Onyx made an extra tiny stride, then he jumped awkwardly, but he got over. Then he galloped to the second one, jumped perfectly out of stride, and made a small circle and came back to us. Peter Finneran said, "Scary, wasn't it?" He pointed to the triple bar. "Well, my heart is in my throat every time you girls head down to a fence. If your parents aren't passing out with anxiety, they're fools. But then, buying you these horses was pretty foolish, so maybe they are fools."

He got off Black George and onto Eileen's bay, then did the same thing, right down the line. Standing there watching Pie in the Sky do this, "chip," did not make me want to jump anything, but I had to admit his second jump was bold and graceful. After I was back on (and I had to mount from the ground—no leg up from Peter Finneran), he sent us to the rail again, and we practiced shortening and lengthening our canter strides—eight strides short, ten strides long, seven strides short, twelve strides long, six strides short, four strides long. There was a lot of barking about where had we learned to count and what was wrong with schools today.

When we started jumping, Pie in the Sky and I had to go first. Peter Finneran pointed to one of the fence posts and said, "You begin your canter there, and you get to that fence in four medium strides, and jump the first one, then four more strides to the second one. Easy as can be."

I sat up, put my heels down, and did what Peter Finneran said. Four strides to the first fence was a little bouncy, four strides to the second fence was a little gallopy, but Pie in the Sky had no trouble, and he didn't even seem to think of stopping. Each horse after me had a slightly different starting spot and a slightly different count, but we all got the job done. He nodded the first four of us through. Then for Sophia it was "One! Two! Three! Sophia! Where are you? You are half a stride off. That horse is a saint, the way he saves you every time! Try it again! Try it again!" After the fourth try, all of which looked okay to me, Sophia began to look rattled. I could see that her eyes were red. Peter Finneran said, "Well, goodness. Go to the back of the line and ponder your sins."

The next exercise was over a hogsback set in the center of the arena, also pretty high—gallop toward it on an angle, jump, gallop away, loop around, and come back at the opposite angle. I thought I would have to pay attention to Pie in the Sky's canter lead, but not at all—he did his own leads. All I had to do was make sure he was level. In this exercise, Margie's horse ran out to the right, but really, it was the easier thing to do. All Peter Finneran said was "Try again," and she did, and she jumped it. As for Sophia, I don't know why she looked down going over the fence, but she did, and even though Onyx performed every step correctly, Sophia got yelled at for three minutes about the first thing you ever learn about riding a horse, and how looking down is falling down, and did he need to tie her braids under her chin to remind her of the most basic rule? I almost asked Eileen if Peter Finneran had yelled at Sophia like this in every class, but I didn't dare, because his hearing was like radar.

We did two more exercises, one with a curving line—a vertical curving five strides to an in-and-out, which made us really sit up and ask the horse to shorten his stride and make it bouncy. The other was a five-fence grid of steep crossbars, which Pie in the Sky greeted like an old friend. For these two exercises, Peter Finneran didn't say much, though once in a while he pretended to be appalled at Margie. Then we were given a course that added all of these exercises together except for the crossbar grid. At the third fence, Pie in the Sky began to stiffen, but I lifted the rein on the stiff side and bent him a little, and he smoothed out and jumped nicely. He was no trouble over the others. Margie's horse was getting tired—he knocked down some poles. Eileen's horse went nicely, and Dinah's horse was, as Peter Finneran said, "workmanlike."

Sophia and Onyx fell apart. I had never seen them make so many mistakes—wrong lead approaching the first jump, and then Sophia panicked about that and tried to change it, so he changed in the front and not in the back. For the curving line, his curve was flat, so he got into the jump wrong and chipped, then he broke to the trot in front of the in-and-out, though he got through it okay. Sophia even said "Dammit!" at one point. When she was finished with all the jumps, she jumped off Onyx the way she always did, leg over the neck, and stomped out of the arena, pulling him behind her.

Peter Finneran said, "One down, four to go."

Pie in the Sky and I were standing next to him, and I said, "You need to mind your manners."

Well, it just came out. I wasn't even thinking it. That was a phrase Daddy used all the time about any child who was getting out of hand, even if the child was not actually his. So instead of me saying it, I like to think that Daddy was speaking through me. Nevertheless, Peter Finneran looked up and me and said, "Who asked you?"

We stared at each other for just a moment, and I thought, I dare you to make *me* cry.

He walked away. After a moment, he looked at his watch and said, "Ten more minutes, girls. Let's try to use them productively."

In fact, our last exercise, pairs abreast, was fun. Pairs abreast was a hunter thing they did in the East—the exhibitors dressed in their complete show hunter outfits, including flask and whip, and rode a whole course right beside each other. I was put with Margie, whose horse was about the same size as Pie in the Sky, and Eileen and Dinah went together. We didn't have any turns—we just trotted and then cantered to three jumps in a row, trying to stay straight and together. The horses seemed to like it; at least Pie in the Sky was very relaxed. Margie and I almost did the thing you were supposed to do, which was be exactly at the top of the jump at the same time. Eileen and Dinah looked nervous, but then they found that it was easier than it looked. After they were finished, it was three thirty, and we had to line up in front of Peter Finneran and hear what he had to say. To me he said, "Abby, you have a nice seat and following hands. Your leg position could be more secure, and your hair could be neater. This horse is preferable to that worthless beast you rode yesterday." Then he turned away.

I did not say a word other than "fine, fine, fine, fine" to Mom, Dad, Danny, or Jane about the Peter Finneran clinic. In fact, I decided to put it out of my mind and never think about it or about him again. I did say a word or two about it to Blue, though. Every time I petted him or gave him a treat, I said, "You are a good boy, and a beauty, and you have the world's most delicious canter." When I got out to the stables on Saturday morning, there was no sign that Peter Finneran had ever been there, and I thought that was good. I gave Ellen and Melinda, whom I hadn't seen since the show, their lessons, and I was really nice to them. Then Mom took me to that store and bought me the black-and-white dress with the short sleeves, because it had been marked down to thirty dollars and she thought that it looked so good that I could wear it around the house if I had to. She put her hands on my shoulders and said, "Wearing nice dresses takes a little practice, you know."

"What do you mean?"

She smiled. "Well, you have to learn not to wipe your hands on your jeans when they get dirty, because sometimes you aren't wearing jeans."

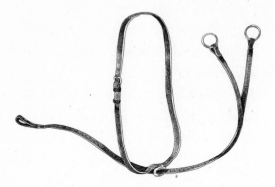

Running Martingale

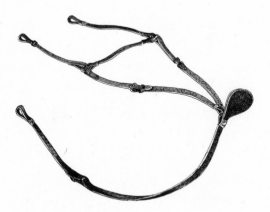

Breastplate

Chapter 6

THEY BROKE US INTO HIGH SCHOOL OVER TWO DAYS AND A night, and every minute of that, I would look around and wonder where the Goldman twins were. They should have been walking down the hall, laughing and talking. They should have been standing with us, looking at the stage in the school theater and planning a recital or a play. They should have been investigating the potter's wheels (two of them) in the art room, and they should have been teasing Mrs. Goldman during the evening meeting in the library, where the principal, Mr. Houston (pronounced HOW-ston, not HEW-ston), was telling us the rules: no short skirts, no cigarettes or chewing tobacco anywhere on the grounds, no beer, only seniors can drive cars, every absence must be excused, have to pass the swimming test, no more than three library books checked out at one time, no writing in textbooks, three tardies equals an absence, three absences results in detention, Saturday detention lasts four hours, one sport per year is required of all students otherwise physical education is mandatory, pick up your PE uniform at the concession stand, and Go, Condors! The school mascot was the California condor, and a huge picture of a condor, painted by someone, hung in the hallway. Also in the hallways were giant pictures of every graduating class, with the class of 1933 by the side door, facing the class of 1966 across the hall. The class of 1933 had had 42 students, 20 girls and 22 boys. The class of 1966 had 356 students from all over the western part of the county. Our little eighth grade that I had gone to school with for three years sort of scattered among the others like sand thrown into the ocean. The Goldman twins, somehow, would have made sure that we didn't disappear.

The surprise was that Sophia was there. I'd thought that she went to private school. When I saw her at the evening meeting, sitting next to a nicely dressed woman who looked just like her, I realized that never had I seen Sophia's mother. I saw Sophia again in assembly the next day, where we were told about student government (one thing we had to do as a class was elect two representatives to the student council, and some other stuff that I didn't understand). High school was about following rules, and we even had a handbook that told us what the rules were. It was twenty pages long.

When you are in eighth grade, you think you are pretty grown-up and all you need to do, really, is get your parents to let you do whatever you want. When you get to ninth grade, it is so obvious that you are not grown-up and that if your parents were to let you do whatever you wanted, the school and the police would stop you anyway. The high school had guards in uniforms—only two of them, but they must have been there to make sure that the older kids did what they were told.

The older kids were the show. There were all types of them, and they controlled the hallways and the pathways of the whole school. In one place, there would be a girl with perfectly set blond hair, standing with her back against the wall and her books in her arms, giggling, with a guy leaning toward her, his hand on the wall behind her head and a pencil in his mouth like a cigarette. Or four guys with hair almost to their shoulders would be lounging under a tree talking about waves and tides. Or a couple would be holding hands in a corner and when you walked past them they would drop hands. Or three guys would be standing in the parking lot by an old car with the hood up, staring at the engine. There were guys with crew cuts and girls with pageboys and girls with hair to their waists and boys with big heads of fluffy curls and girls with big heads of fluffy curls and even boys with mustaches and chin whiskers. There were girls dressed like me, in plain skirts and blouses, and there were girls in dresses that looked like swirls of flower colors, girls in peasant blouses, and even two boys in old suits, but they were barefoot.

When we got into our classes (I was taking English, geometry, ancient history, geology, French, and tennis), all the kids in the ninth grade looked a little scared and not as colorful, and it was sort of a relief. I hoped that Daddy would never come to the high school—it would be a big shock for him.

Mom was the one who came to the evening meeting. She didn't say much, but she laughed a few times. I thought she enjoyed herself. She said, "Well, goodness me. When did Danny start here? Was that four years ago or forty? It's not the same place at all."

Sophia was in my ancient history class, Gloria was in my geology class and my geometry class, and Stella was in my English class. Of the other kids, Kyle was in history, geology, and geometry; Larry Schnuck was in English, where the male teacher wore big glasses and looked old, so I figured Larry would cause a lot of trouble; and Leslie was in French and tennis. Leslie had been at camp all summer—she hadn't even been home by the time of Barbie and Alexis's big party, so no one had laid eyes on her in months. She looked much happier and taller. She had also learned how to do something with her hair. She brushed it straight back, under a tortoiseshell headband. It hung below her shoulders and was very shiny. I saw Kyle Gonzalez bump into her and excuse himself as if he had never seen her before. Then she and I exchanged a glance, and she rolled her eyes. I laughed. My plan for high school was to stay out of the way and do my homework on the way home on the bus. The ride was about ten minutes longer than the old bus ride, so time at home would be short. Most of the high school kids lived in town, which meant that we were the country bumpkins, and so we had to keep our eyes open and our mouths shut.

Riding Oh My, Blue, and Nobby was the best part of the day.

I didn't get back to real work with Blue until the Friday after school started. I had let him take a break for four days after the clinic, and then we went on the trail a few times. He seemed fine, and as happy to forget Peter Finneran as I was. But Friday was an early day—we got home from school before three—so Daddy had set up some jumps in the arena to see what Blue had learned. There were hay bales, two verticals, and a gate Daddy had put together out of tree branches, actually a very handsome jump—about 2'6", with an X surrounded by a frame, like a regular gate, though the tree branches curved a little and were covered with bark. I thought the stables should have one.

We did all the things I normally did—work him in the round corral, both directions at the trot and the canter, plenty of turns and plenty of stepping over. Then I got on him in the arena and trotted him in figure eights and small circles and serpentines, backed him, walked him, cantered and did some lead changes. Daddy was standing in the middle, and he didn't tell me what to do—Blue was my horse and my business. But Daddy was smiling. After our flat work, I felt good.

Blue had jumped all the jumps in the arena more than once, and over the summer, Daddy had even done what he liked especially to do—put strange things on the jumps, books and stuffed animals and dangling spoons, to get Blue used to surprises. Blue had never been as calm about the surprises as Black George had been, but he got so he didn't mind them. Today, though, there were no surprises—Daddy had been doing errands all day with no time to think up tricks.

Nevertheless, Blue was a mess.

As he trotted down to the first vertical, his ears seemed to go farther forward than possible, and then he tossed his head and refused. Not only that, but after refusing, he backed up a couple of steps. Daddy said, "What was that?" He looked around, then said, "His eyes are popping out of his head." But there was nothing on the hillside, nothing outside the fence,, not even really a breeze. I turned him and tried again. This time I was prepared and made him jump the fence, which he did, but he seemed more nervous about it than he had ever been. Daddy put the jump down, and instead of jumping, we trotted over the three poles lying together between the standards. It took us four times of that for him to calm down. Then Daddy raised the poles about a foot, and we trotted through those.

The second vertical was only two feet high, and it looked exactly like the first one, but when we approached it, he did the same thing as he had done before—acted terrified. Well, we could not let him avoid the jump, so we did what we had done with the first one, and worked him over the poles until he was calmer. But after that, I went to Daddy in the center of the arena and said, "That's enough for me. He's scared to death. I don't understand it." Inside, I was thinking about what Peter Finneran had said—maybe Blue was a worthless beast after all.

Daddy said, "Is he seeing ghosts?" I said nothing—this reminded me of the spring, but I had never told Daddy about my ghost fears. "Well, tomorrow is another day, and we'll definitely pray over this. Don't worry about it, okay?"

I nodded. But how was I not going to worry about it?

When we took Oh My and Lady on the trail, Daddy kept pointing out birds (blue jay, hawk, early owl, kingfisher, crows, even a hummingbird), animals (two ground squirrels, a bobcat), and plants (tree moss, olive tree, many oaks with unusual branches, walnut, mustard), and then he had me tell him all about school (I told him about the books were we going to read for class—*The Red Badge of Courage*, *Le Ballon Rouge*, *Introduction to Geometry*, *Mountains and Oceans*, and *The Egyptians*). He was keeping me from worrying about Blue. And I did stop worrying about him and start worrying about geology. Just that very day, our geology teacher, Mr. Mallon, had asked us how old we thought the world ("the Earth") was, and Kyle had given the correct answer, four and a half billion years old, and he knew all about some meteorite that had landed somewhere in Arizona and was tested for something that showed how old the universe was. This was way older than the Bible said, and I was glad I hadn't raised my hand. But then, I planned to never raise my hand.

On Monday, in history, Sophia came in, sat down right next to me as if we were perfectly good friends, and said, "You should ride Pie in the Sky again."

"He was nice."

"He's erratic."

"I liked him." Then I said, "Peter Finneran was kind of mean."

Then the teacher gave us a look, and we opened our textbooks. I watched Sophia for a moment, and I was sorry I had said anything. She stared at the book and began kicking her foot against the leg of her chair. Miss Cumberland said, "Abby Lovitt! Do you have something better to do than read your book?"

I read my book. We had done pharaohs already in seventh grade, but this time we were going to go from Egypt to Ur to

Greece to Rome, all before Thanksgiving. I have to say that the textbook about the Egyptians did not say much about the Israelites, but even so, there were pretty interesting things in there—photographs of pyramids and drawings of tiny little men pushing huge stones up ramps on some logs. There were also a lot of Egyptian paintings of kings, where the kings were very large and the regular people only came up to about their knees. By the end of the period, Sophia was her normal self—she marched off to her next class without looking right or left.

A couple of days later, Miss Cumberland gave us paper and colored pencils—as a project, we were supposed to draw ourselves in the Egyptian way, with the feet and head looking north, say, and the chest looking west. Sophia and I drew each other, and the pictures made us laugh. I gave her a hard hat, big feet, and riding boots, and she gave me a whip in my hand. We gave each other horses that looked sort of Egyptian, too. Miss Cumberland tacked all the drawings to the bulletin board. After that, we talked pretty often, but Sophia never said "Hi," or "Bye," or "See you later." She just started talking or stopped talking, depending on whether she had something to say.

It turned out that she had gone to the private school that ended in eighth grade. Then most of her friends went on to the private high school, but Sophia didn't want such a long day, and Colonel Hawkins agreed with her—the private school started after nine and didn't get out until almost five, whereas the public school started just before eight and got out by three. More time to ride. Sophia and her mom had discussed it all summer, and finally, when Sophia had promised to make all A's (which she had not done at her previous school), her mom had given in. Her dad didn't care—he had gone to our high school, the class of 1943 (one day, after class, she showed me his picture in the hall). Her mom was from Chicago. Her parents had met in the army during the Second World War. She was an only child. She had four dogs—a miniature poodle of her own, two King Charles spaniels that her mom took to dog shows, and a Gordon setter that her dad hunted with. The poodle's best trick was that she could balance a piece of cheese on her nose, then toss it in the air and catch it.

At lunch, I always sat with Gloria and Stella, while Sophia sat with another girl who was her next-door neighbor—they had known each other since they were babies. Gloria and Stella thought that Sophia could do with a makeover. Gloria said that her clothes were fine, "good-quality," so the best thing in the world would be for her to cut her braids and wear her hair in a nice shoulder-length flip—fairly conservative, but with some bounce. That would offset the thinness of her face and emphasize her eyes, which were her best feature. Stella said that Sophia should get herself a padded bra, because her shoulders were so big that she looked like a boy. I did not tell Sophia any of these things. Gloria and Stella got two other girls to sit with us, Mary and Luisa, and Leslie sat with us most of the time, too. I have to say that we all, literally, looked up to Leslie now. She was four inches taller than Stella, who was the tallest, and she confided that the camp had been a weight-loss camp—she had lost twenty pounds and she knew exactly how to keep it off, which was swimming or playing basketball every day of the week. She had lots of opinions, which was not the Leslie I had ever known, but one of the things they had done at her camp was spend two whole days and nights alone, with only a knife, a box of matches, some water, and a blanket. They were supposed to fast and think about their goals and re-name themselves a secret name that they would never reveal, but that was the name of their future self. I noticed that some of the older boys looked at her, too.

I always looked into the mailbox before reaching in, because Brian Connelly had reached into his mailbox in the spring and pulled out a black widow spider. Of course, he knew just what it was because he had seen a show about spiders on TV. It didn't bite him, but he knew that it could, and he told us all about ten times that if he had to choose between being bitten by a black widow and being bitten by a tarantula, he would take the tarantula any day. Thanks to the fact that Brian re-peated this story so much, I always remembered to check, and also to think about tarantulas, wolf spiders, jumping spiders, and all the other spiders Brian had seen on TV. There were no spiders in the mailbox that day, but there was a letter from Bar-bie Goldman, addressed to me, and the envelope was decorated with pictures of faces making all sorts of expressions, from sur-prised to happy to scared to sad. On the back of the envelope were three horse faces, and they were also looking surprised, glad, and sad. I tore open the envelope very carefully, and pulled out the letter. It read:

Dear Abby—

We have now been at the Jackson School for twelve hours. We have built three fires, carried seven buckets of water, fed ten horses, ground some corn into meal, dug a giant hole in the dirt for a latrine, identified seven plants (including poison oak), six species of birds, four species of trees, three types of clouds, and learned the difference between schist and granite. Alexis says that when the pioneers came to California, they skipped the Jackson School, and so it must be our job to set up the homestead and apply for statehood. All the teachers are tall and muscular, and you can't tell the men from the women. Whenever you say, "Mr. So-and-so, how do I do such and such?" Mr. So-and-so says, "Well, Barbara, let's think about that. What do YOU think would be a good way to approach that problem?" And then Mr. So-and-so waits a very long time for you to think up something. It is strange. I do think that Alexis is going to try the patience of every single one of them to the limit, but I haven't warned them. The thing is, if you ask Alexis a question, she asks you a question back, and keeps doing it until you make a statement. It is her METHOD. So we shall see.

I wanted to tell you, though, that I have met my horse. Thanks to you, I have an INTERMEDIATE horse (Alexis's horse is a BEGINNER horse). His name is Tooter, and he is a fifteen-hand roan gelding, ten years old. He is a little boring compared to Blue, whom I MISS TERRIBLY BECAUSE HE IS MY SOUL MATE, but I will make do. I also miss you. I have been separated from Alexis (Mom's doing, I'm sure) and my roommate is an unsuspecting girl from Seattle, Washington, who is the oldest of five, and therefore very well behaved. Her name is Siobhan, which is pronounced "Shevawn." Alexis's roommate is named Ruth. She is from San Francisco. Little do they know.

Our class is small—only sixteen kids, eight boys and eight girls, seventy-two kids in the whole school. I am wondering what it is like at the high school. Maybe you have made ten new friends. I wish I could be in two places at once. Write me back! We are starved for mail.

Love,
Barbara

I stood on the porch reading this. Mom opened the door, looked at me, and asked me if I would like a ham sandwich. I said yes, and right then and there she brought her hand out from behind her back, and gave me a ham sandwich. I laughed. Rusty, who was out in the front yard, barked. I said, "Rusty wants a ham sandwich, too."

Mom smiled fondly. "Ah, she is spoiled rotten, that dog. I've done a wonderful job." She went back into the house. I hadn't expected to get any letters from Barbie—I felt like she had vanished into thin air—so now there was something to look forward to.

I went into the kitchen. I showed Mom the envelope of Barbie's letter, and she said, "Speaking of self-confidence . . ." We laughed. Then I went up to my room, carefully cut the envelope open so you could see both sides, and tacked it to my bulletin board, right beside the envelope for the invitation.

* * *

It was either the next afternoon or the one after that that Stella was called to the principal's office. We were sitting outside at the end of the day, waiting for the buses, and the secretary came down the stairs and tapped her on the shoulder. Stella was still in there when the buses came, so Gloria promised to call me that night. I knew it would be something bad from the look on Miss Harris's face, so that evening I did my homework in the living room, in the chair closest to the phone. If I answered and sounded casual, then I would be able to talk for ten minutes and would find out what was going on. If Daddy answered, then he would say that I was studying and I would have to talk to Gloria tomorrow. One of Daddy's principles was that anything that we girls might discuss could wait.

It worked, because when the phone rang, Dad had gone into the kitchen for a glass of water, and Mom was counting stitches in her knitting pattern and said, "Abby, why don't you get that?"

I picked it up. Gloria whispered, "She was smoking a cigarette in the girls' bathroom."

I said, "Oh, yes, I did write down that assignment."

Gloria knew perfectly well that my parents were in the room with me. She went on, "Somebody turned her in. She said that someone was in a stall, but she doesn't know who, just that she was wearing white Keds. So we are supposed to look at everyone's shoes."

I said, "Chapter three, and answer the questions at the end."

Gloria said, "She doesn't really like cigarettes, they're for weight control. One before every meal."

I said, "It's not due until Monday."

Gloria said, "But it's kind of my fault."

I thought it was safe to say, "In what way?"

"Because I lit them for her for the first week she was trying them, back in July. She was afraid of matches, and she got me to light them, and now she's hooked. She says she's not, but she is."

I said, "Excuse me?"

"She's suspended for three days."

Daddy said, "Ten minutes is up."

I said, "Got to go."

Gloria understood. I guess the main reason that Gloria stayed my best friend was that she understood everything about my family and didn't care.

That night when I went to bed, I remembered that I had seen Stella and Gloria the night of the Goldmans' party, out on the big back deck. They were over in a corner, and I might have seen a flash. I hadn't thought anything about it, because Gloria had come into the house a moment later and started dancing with Brian Connelly. Stella didn't come in for a long time after that. It hadn't even occurred to me to wonder where she was, but I bet Gloria knew.

My own opinion was that it wasn't all that bad to have Stella gone for three days. When we were eating our lunch, we didn't talk so much about what the other girls looked like or what they were wearing. Leslie was more in charge when Stella was gone, so we talked about which of the junior boys was the cutest. We didn't dare talk about the senior boys, though. We also didn't talk about Stella.

* * *

Carlie Hollingsworth, who went to our church, was now in high school, too, and our high schools were number one rivals. This actually made us better friends because we had something to talk about, the Condors and the Coyotes. Mr. Hollingsworth had played football in both high school and college, as something called an "end," which Carlie said was the boy on the team who was always running somewhere and trying to catch the pass. Mr. Hollingsworth was thrilled that he could now be a big fan of the Coyotes, and even more thrilled that the Coyotes had been first in the league the year before (the Condors had been third). The first game, with a team called the Range Riders, had ended at 21–0 in favor of the Coyotes, of course. I knew that the Condors had lost their first game 0–6, but I knew only because Gloria had gone with Leslie and called to tell me. Carlie knew this without me telling her. She rolled her eyes and said, "Pop is a little nuts."

My dad didn't even know that the name of our team was the Condors. I guessed that Mr. Hollingsworth would tell him. Also, one good thing about Mr. Hollingsworth going to the games was that he saw what the other kids had on compared to Carlie, and on the way home, he stopped at a store and bought her some nice clothes. She was wearing a new dress to church. It had long sleeves and a collar like the collar of a man's shirt, but it was short—the hem was a few inches above her knees. I could see the Sisters glancing at it and making noises, but I liked it, and I thought she looked pretty. Daddy, who had learned his lesson with the Greeleys, acted as if he didn't notice the dress, and Mom went right up to her and said, "That's a sweet dress, Carlie! I love the collar."

Mrs. Hollingsworth said, "Why they would put long sleeves on a short dress I will never understand. Too hot in the summer and too cold in the winter." Simultaneously, she shook her head and Carlie rolled her eyes. Brother Abner gave a talk about "the Rules and the Spirit." When we had our supper, which was meatloaf made by Mrs. Hollingsworth, I saw Mrs. Larkin and Mom off in a corner, talking for a long time, but when Daddy looked over at them, they stopped talking. I thought that was weird.

Oxer Jump

Mounting Block

Chapter 7

AFTER OUR ONE JUMPING SESSION WITH DADDY, I'D TRIED TO forget the whole thing. I had ridden in the arena, down to the crick, up the hillside, and down the road. I had gone out with Mom, with Dad, with Danny, and by myself. Blue had been kind and responsible—one time, when Morning Glory shied with Mom at a deer, Blue just stood there and let Morning Glory bump into him. He hadn't minded the cows up the hill—not blue Brahmas this time, just plain old Herefords. He had gone nicely into the water in the crick (just a ripple, though), and up and down the banks. He had walked on a loose rein and trotted out when asked. He hadn't even minded Rusty weaving in and out of the trees—he was used to Rusty, and Dad would say that a horse knows where its dog is every minute, just like he would have his eye on the neighborhood wolves if there were any.

In the arena and in the pen, I had set out poles for him to trot over, and he had done so, only looking down at them every so often. But it wasn't my idea to jump him. I just came home from school and found a couple of jumps set up, Blue wearing his English saddle, and Daddy ready to go. He had made four jumps—a vertical of poles, his branch gate, an oxer of poles, and a row of hay bales. They were set with one end against the fence rail, so there'd be no run-outs in that direction. After we worked Blue in the pen so that he was relaxed, we led him around the arena and sat or leaned on the jumps and petted him so that he was more relaxed. Then I stepped him over about a zillion times so that he was as relaxed as he could be, and I have to say that when I got on him and we walked, trotted, and cantered, he seemed good. But when I turned him toward that first vertical, I felt his body go rigid and I had to kick him over the fence, which he took awkwardly.

Daddy walked over and gave me a whip. He said, "Don't hit him, just make sure he knows you have it."

I took it in my hand lash upward, like a weapon, the way Peter Finneran said, and headed for the fence. Blue sped up so much I had to really take hold because I was afraid he would run away. Once again, he threw himself over the jump. I dropped the whip. Daddy picked it up and said, "What did you learn in that clinic? Peter Finneran said you have to make him do it."

"But when I do that, it feels like he doesn't know what he's doing. He might run into the fence or fall down."

"Peter Finneran is the expert on jumping, not me. He showed you how to press him."

"I don't believe him."

Daddy shook his head—only a tiny bit, the way you do when you are getting exasperated.

I said, "I mean, I don't believe him about Blue. He hated Blue."

"No horseman hates a horse."

"He said he was a worthless beast. That's why he put me on Pie in the Sky."

"I'm sure he was just—" But then he stopped. What was there to say? Daddy pursed his lips. Then he said, "Well, that was not something he should have said to a child who paid thirty dollars to ride in his clinic."

I said, "You paid?"

"Well, we paid thirty. Jane gave you thirty for coaching the girls in the show, so the other kids paid sixty."

"Sophia paid sixty dollars to have him yell at her for three days?"

"All of you girls paid money to be coached by the best in the business."

I said, "Well, he didn't like Blue, and I don't think he understood him."

"I don't think we understand him, either."

I said, "Yes, but we like him."

Daddy said, "Well, then he's a lucky horse. Why don't you walk him around for a while, and take him up the hill. He enjoys that. Let's say he's just not a jumper, all right? There's nothing wrong with that."

I nodded.

That evening, after I did my homework and finished *The Red Badge of Courage*, I decided to write Barbie a letter:

Dear Mlle. Barbara Goldman:

There is one thing wrong with our high school and it is that you and Alexis are not there! (Maybe that is two things.) But you should see Leslie. She went to a camp for losing weight (and she is the first one to tell you that), and now she swims and is taller than everyone else. She looks really good, and she knows it, and I told Gloria when she said that that there is nothing wrong with her knowing it. Better that than doing what Stella does all the time, which is to tell you how terrible she looks today, but hoping that you will tell her that she is wrong, which I always do because I am afraid not to.

And guess what? Stella started smoking cigarettes, and she smoked one in the girls' bathroom and got caught, so she was suspended for three days. She's back now, and every time she opens her purse, she makes sure that you see that the pack of cigarettes is in there—Pell Mell or something like that.

I think you would like the high school. They have already cast the first school play—it is The Crucible, *and how they can do it without you I don't know. It is perfect for high school because freshmen have to play the girls who see the ghosts, and there are lots of girls' parts—ten or eleven. I guess last spring they did* Peter Pan *and there were about three girls' parts, so the audience wasn't very big. You would love the theater. There is room for a BIG audience.*

Also, there are two plays each year directed by students. Will that make you come home?

Right after you left, I did a riding clinic with a very famous man named Peter Finneran, who was in the Olympics and everything. I guess by the time he was my age, he was already a U.S. champion rider, and he is not that old now. Thirty, if that. Anyway, he hated Blue, and called him a worthless beast. And yes, it is totally true that Blue cost me five dollars and sixty cents and the other horse I rode cost thousands of dollars, but since you love Blue, I am telling you this because it really bothers me, and even though I actually had fun in the clinic sometimes, because he was really good at thinking up exercises, it makes me mad every time I remember it. There was another girl in the clinic named Sophia who we didn't know (she went to the Derby School through eighth grade). She's now at the high school, and I sort of think she's my friend. This man was as mean to her as kids at school are when they are doing their worst—I am thinking THE BIG FOUR! I should ask her about it but I'm afraid to.

So anyway, I do wonder how you are doing there. I hope it's not really three campfires and twelve buckets of water a day. But your horse Tooter sounds nice! Just remember to keep your heels down and your eyes up and your you-know-what deep in the saddle. You are a good rider, and Blue misses you! You can ride him as much as you want when you come home for vacation, if they let you do that.

Je t'aime,
Abby

113

The next day was my birthday, but even if Sophia had known that, I wouldn't have expected her to notice. She plopped herself down in front of me in ancient history (now we were working on Mesopotamia) and said to me, "I am going to stare at you until you say you'll come ride Pie in the Sky this weekend."

I stared back at her, but I could not keep myself from laughing, and so I said I would ask Mom.

She said, "I know you teach those girls, and I know you do it at nine, so I will have Rodney saddle Pie in the Sky for ten thirty."

She kept staring at me, even when Miss Cumberland said, "Sophia! Can you explain the difference between the Akkadians and the Babylonians?"

But Sophia continued to stare at me until I nodded. Maybe this was twenty seconds, but it seemed like five minutes. Then she turned to Miss Cumberland, and said, "The Babylonians were in the south and the Akkadians were in the north."

Miss Cumberland said, "Well, not exactly, but—" Then she went on to say that there was a myth the Sumerians had about a huge flood like the flood in the Bible with Noah's Ark. I thought this was interesting. There was also a long story called *The Epic of Gilgamesh*. Miss Cumberland got excited about this story and passed around some photographs of the clay tablets that the story was written on. There were ten of them, and people had only been able to read them for about a hundred years because a man who Miss Cumberland said was a great hero had translated them even though he hardly had any education and taught himself almost everything he knew. Miss Cumberland was going to ditto some parts of the epic for us to read in the next few days. At one point, Kyle Gonzales raised his hand and said that clay tablets were a great invention, as great as the wheel, because all you had to do to write on them was press a reed into them and move it a little bit.

Miss Cumberland kept nodding, and I could tell that Kyle was going to get an A in ancient history, but that would never be enough for him. What he really wanted to do was be up there at the teacher's desk, telling us what he knew. Miss Cumberland said, "Kyle, I know you like to find out things."

Kyle said, "A man came by and sold my mom an *Encyclopaedia Britannica*, and it is the best set of books ever written."

Some of the boys opened their mouths and rolled their heads around like this was a dumb thing to say, but Miss Cumberland didn't even notice them.

At lunch, Leslie and Gloria pulled out a Snickers bar and two candles, and Leslie used her fork to dig two little holes in the Snickers. They pushed the candles in, and Stella actually took out a match and lit them. I blew them out in exactly one second, and what I wished for was a good ride on Pie in the Sky on Saturday. There were no presents, but Gloria invited me to her house Friday night for a small party. And it was fun— Leslie, Gloria, Stella, Mary, and Luisa were there, and they gave me some nice things, like a Simon and Garfunkel album and a Gary Lewis and the Playboys album. Gloria also gave me a scarf that her mother had knitted for me, though Gloria had done a few inches. It was blue and yellow, Condors colors.

Leslie gave me a book called *Smoke Rings*, and Stella gave me some blue eye shadow, certainly a hint. When I got home, I found out why Mom had insisted that I not stay out too late. Even though she and Dad had already given me a new winter coat on the actual day of my birthday, while I was out at the party, they had put a new hi-fi set in my room, on the bookcase, and Mom, Dad, and Danny had each given me a record. Danny picked the Lovin' Spoonful, Mom picked the Mamas and the Papas, and Daddy picked the Statler Brothers. And then I got to listen, with the sound turned down, until I fell asleep. I actually felt fourteen.

On Saturday, I put on my good riding clothes and my new boots even though it was hot at our house—seventy-two and only eight thirty in the morning. Mom gave me two dollars as a tip for Rodney and said that he deserved more, but this would be enough for now. I put it in the pocket of my breeches. Mom had agreed to pick me up at noon—she had something that she wanted to discuss with Sister Larkin anyway, and what with going to the store and getting her hair cut, the extra time was fine. The surprise was that it was hot at the stables, too, and sunny in a way that you almost never saw there. "Except in October," said Jane. For Melinda, I made up a sort of horse scavenger hunt. I got a couple of carrots from a bucket Jane had and broke them into small pieces, then I went around the grounds of the stables—sometimes even a little bit into the woods—and set them places that Melinda could reach from the saddle—on top of a fence post or on a stump or a tree branch or the hood of a car, and I sent Melinda and Gallant

Man to find them. If they got lost, I shouted "hot" or "cold." Each time Melinda found one, she would lean forward and hand it to Gallant Man, which made her practice leaning forward and gave him a reason to limber up by turning to look at her. I could see by the end of the exercise that Gallant Man was looking for the carrots, too. I would never put it past a pony to understand the point of a game, especially a food game.

This game meant that when Ellen showed up to jump, Gallant Man was fresh and ready. For Ellen, I set the jumps the way Peter Finneran had that first day—eighteen inches high, in a big X—so that she would get plenty of practice turning and coming back to the jump from both directions. Ellen liked this exercise, just the way that she liked every complicated exercise better than every simple exercise—she had to think about it and didn't have time to complain. She did a good job, too, which she told me all about as we walked back to the barn. One thing about Ellen was that it didn't matter whether I praised her, because she always praised herself. Most of the time she was right—she never said that she had done something correctly when she had done it wrong. It was like she was making a list in her head of all the things she did do right, so that she would remember them, and why not?

Rodney, Colonel Hawkins, Jane, and Sophia were standing there with Black George and Pie in the Sky when I got back to the barn. Ellen dismounted, and I handed her her pony, then I went over to the hook where I had hung my hard hat. Ellen said, "Can I watch?" And Jane said, "Your mother is waiting. Maybe next week."

Next week?

Sophia said, "Was it your birthday?"

I nodded.

But she didn't say anything else. Jane said, "Happy birthday."

Rodney gave me a leg up onto Pie in the Sky, and Colonel Hawkins took Black George over to the mounting block and got on. He led the way to the big arena, and Jane and Sophia walked behind us. I tried not to turn around and stare. I had never seen Colonel Hawkins ride Black George or any other horse. It was Jane who gave the lesson. Sophia stood near her in the center of the arena, watching.

When I had been on Pie in the Sky for about five minutes, I knew all through my body that what Danny and I had done with him on the day I rode him in the clinic had made a big difference in him. This horse was prancy and stiff, and he tossed his head about six times. He also decided that two of the cars parked beside the big arena were not to be trusted, and though he didn't shy, he curved out away from them when we passed them. Was there something going on in the woods? Better look. Was there something going on up the road? Better look. He felt like a mess. But Jane hadn't given any commands yet; she was still watching us, so in a fairly open part of the arena, where there weren't any jumps, I had him step over three times in each direction, and then bend to the left and bend to the right. I remembered Danny doing some spirals, and did two of those in each direction. Still Jane didn't say anything, so I realized that they had decided to let me do it my way. He stopped feeling like a mess and began feeling just a little "untidy," as the teachers would say. But that was an improvement. I enjoyed him. He had a bouncy trot and a light mouth.

Jane said, "Are we all warmed up?"

Colonel Hawkins said, "A brisk hand gallop would be good for them." He got up in his stirrups and off they went.

Colonel Hawkins did not ride like a soldier, which surprised me. His stirrups were long and his feet were pushed pretty far into them. His knees were pretty straight. He also kind of bent his back instead of doing that soldier thing, which is spine straight, chin up, shoulders down, yes sir. But even so, he went right along with Onyx on a light rein, quiet in the saddle. In the meantime, Pie in the Sky was enjoying himself, and kicked up now and then. I didn't mind that. I knew it would loosen his back. It is funny how every horse feels completely different from every other horse. Just watching Onyx, I remembered how Black George had felt—smooth and solid and steady. He was happy to do his work and always willing, but he wasn't catlike or loose. You could sense froom the way he used his body that he was thinking and planning. That's why jumping big jumps was not as hard as it might seem—he always knew where he was, and because he was big and solid, where he was was where he was going to stay. He was reliable, and also talented. We got a lot of money for him because those two things don't always go together.

Pie in the Sky felt different. The power he had was not steady and solid power, but whooshing and energetic. Sometimes the power felt disorganized and sort of outside of him, and then sometimes, like when I started galloping with Colonel Hawkins, that power arranged itself and just came through him from back to front; you were sitting on it and going with it. There was not a solid thing between me and Pie in the Sky's feet—I felt his feet, each stride, come up through him and enter me. My hips opened and closed, my shoulders and elbows followed his stride, he loosened me up. I could not say which horse felt better, just that they were entirely different, and different, too, from Blue, who was not as powerful as Pie in the Sky, but more floating, as if with each stride he was in the air a little longer. After our gallop, which didn't last nearly long enough, I did what Colonel Hawkins did with Onyx, and brought Pie in the Sky down to a walk. We walked around Jane and Sophia while Jane gave us our first course.

There is no horse, even a champion, who doesn't need a warm-up, so she pointed us to a vertical a little off by itself, with canter poles in front of it, and we cantered that three times, then we went around the end of the arena and came back toward the center over a small gate. Then we did those two again, adding a right turn to a small oxer, and so on, building a course jump by jump. The jumps started about 2'9" and went to about 3'3". The horses seemed to enjoy it—they maintained a good pace, and all I really had to do with Pie in the Sky was keep him level in the turns. Over one oxer he jumped me out of the saddle—his arc was so high that I felt bounced, but then he came down straight, so I just came down with him and galloped on. I lost a stirrup, but found it on the turn.

Colonel Hawkins never lost a stirrup—his feet and legs were as steady as if he were just standing there. But he didn't go very far forward over the top—he sort of curled but stayed fairly deep in the saddle. Jane must have seen me looking at him, so she walked over and put her hand on Pie in the Sky's shoulder and said, "You didn't know that Colonel Hawkins was a three-day rider, did you?"

"No. What's that?"

"Oh, it's an old army thing, but it's in the Olympics. The first day is dressage, the second day is cross-country, which is sort of like foxhunting, though more technical, and the third day is show jumping, with pretty high jumps but not really high jumps. Anyway, the horses and the riders have to be all-around athletes, so it's very demanding."

"Is that why he doesn't ride like the pictures in the book?"

"Which book?"

"That cavalry manual with the drawings I saw at the show."

"Probably. In cross-country people tend to sit back a little more and ride defensively. The jumps are often quite intimidating."

"Like on our outside course?"

"Oh, except for the water, those are very tame. Someday we'll go down toward the ocean, through the woods, and you can see the big ones."

"Do we have to jump them?"

She laughed. I took this as a no.

In the meantime, Colonel Hawkins was doing his course, kind of a serpentine with an in-and-out and then a wall at the end. Black George made it look easy, and Sophia just stared at him. She did not join in our conversation or even look in our direction.

Now it was my turn. I felt no stiffness in Pie in the Sky, but I did a little figure eight anyway, pushing him to the outside with my leg so that he softened and bent in each direction before approaching the jump. They were all about 3'6". I eased from the figure eight into a circle and headed for the first fence. I thought all the right thoughts: look up, aim for the center, sit up, look beyond the jump, stay level. As we got near the first jump, I looked for the second one, which was off to the left. Pie in the Sky leapt, then landed and eased into the turn. His strides were big but bouncy. He galloped to number two, and I was staring at number three, a solid coop. But when we got to three, it was like Pie in the Sky was saying, "Show me something I care about." He was also galloping like he was on a railroad track—no question about the turns or the line to the jump, everything put together as if it were one single thing, not a bunch of things, or maybe one single thought, not a bunch of separate thoughts. I saw and I felt that for Pie in the Sky getting over the jumps was automatic, but making a course of it was the challenge. If one thing led to another, then he was fine and happy. For this course, one thing led to another to another and to another. It was not like any course I had ever ridden. Black George had always made it simple, but Pie in the Sky seemed to take it very seriously, and to want to do it just right. He did it just right. I sort of felt my hair standing on end, if that is possible when you are wearing a hard hat.

Jane was smiling, and Sophia was staring at us. Colonel Hawkins said, "Well, let's walk these boys out. They did a good job. Let's take them over to the outside course." Colonel Hawkins put Onyx on a loose rein; I didn't feel quite comfortable doing the same with Pie in the Sky, because he was looking around with his ears pricked. As he followed along behind Onyx, I started to wonder how it was that I could do so well on Pie and so badly on Blue. If you are a good rider, you are supposed to be able to ride everyone; if your horse is a good horse, he is supposed to be good for everyone. We walked along behind Onyx as Colonel Hawkins did what grown-ups do. He walked up to each of the jumps and gave it a once-over, just to see what needed to be fixed. He didn't say anything to me. Pretty soon, both horses were cooled out and ready to be put away. We went back to the barn, where Rodney cross-tied Onyx, and then came and held Pie in the Sky while I dismounted. Sophia was nowhere to be seen. I handed Rodney the two dollars, and he said, "Well, that's a kind remembrance, lass."

Jane came out of one of the stalls a little way down the row and said, "Ah, Abby! I think you've got time to have a little chat. Come on to my office."

"What time is it?"

"Eleven thirty."

"That didn't take long."

"The colonel likes a brisk half hour better than a lazy hour. But these are trained horses, and the show season is over. We need to keep them in moderate fitness, but not to drill them."

I followed her around the end of the barn. When I was sure no one was nearby, I said, "Why didn't Sophia ride Onyx?"

"Oh, me. She's not saying."

"Is she afraid?"

"I would not have ever thought she could be, and if she is, she isn't acting like it. She comes out dressed to ride, and watches Colonel Hawkins, every step, then goes home. He doesn't know what's going on, either."

"Does he ride Pie in the Sky, too?"

"Yes, or Rodney takes one or the other of them on a trail. A 'walkabout,' he calls it, which is Australian—don't know why he would use that word, but he puts us on."

"I thought Rodney didn't ride anymore."

"Oh, he does what we call riding—he gets up on the horses and takes them out. He doesn't do what he calls riding, which is go hell-bent for leather over large obstacles in a state of ine-briation. In England they call it steeple chasing, but I just call it madness. You did a good job on Pie in the Sky. He's not an easy horse."

"It was kind of amazing."

"Yes, when he is good, he is very very good, but when he is bad, he is horrid."

"Jem Jarrow should work with him."

"That's your friend."

I raised my voice just a tiny bit, in order to be emphatic, because Jane just seemed to be talking idly as if none of this really mattered. "Jem Jarrow could help him get himself orga-nized. That's what I was thinking when we had our round. All the parts came together. He's not playing. Black G—I mean Onyx—is playing. But Pie in the Sky worries too much to play."

Jane looked at me, then said, "Well, that is an intelligent analysis." She smiled.

I said, "Is Pie in the Sky so good because he was expensive?"

Jane made a little quick smile, and then said, "Talent is al-ways expensive and he has a good show record."

"Was he from the East, like the mare?"

"No. He was from LA."

"Was he more than five dollars and sixty cents?"

Jane grinned. "Wasn't that thirty-five cents? I was sure there were two nickels in there. Abby, dear, the circumstances of your purchase of True Blue do not reflect his potential. But, yes, Pie in the Sky was a lucky fellow—he was bred to jump, and then he was taught to jump, and he jumps. His trainer is a bit of a legend, and it isn't always the case that a new owner can get the same thing out of one of that trainer's horses that that trainer got out of him. But everyone was aware of that going in."

I didn't know how to ask for the price—and Mom would have been horrified if I had—but I did say, "Maybe more than Onyx?"

Jane said, "Maybe."

They had paid ten thousand dollars for Onyx, though I wasn't supposed to know that.

We stood there.

For the first time in all the times I had come into Jane's office, I noticed that there was a row of books on a shelf above her desk. I remembered that cavalry manual, so now I looked around for a moment and said, "Please, could I look at your books?"

"The riding books?" She glanced at them.

I nodded.

"Help yourself. But it's chaos." She pulled one down and said, "The Littauer is good. The colonel knows him. He's very down to earth." She handed me a rather thin volume, with a blue and tan cover, *Schooling Your Horse*—one of those books

I'd seen in the tent at the show. "But look at the others, too. Now I have to go get ready for another lesson. It's ten of twelve."

She went to the door and opened it, then she turned and said, "You were good on that horse. Maybe you should write Mr. Jarrow's number down for me."

"I don't have it, but Danny does. I'll call you."

Jane nodded and went out.

I have to say that I walked slowly to the parking lot. First I went by Pie in the Sky's stall. I petted him on the right cheek and on the left, then I tickled his forehead around his swirl. He seemed to enjoy it. But I was not going to start liking this horse, because he would never be mine. As Daddy always told me, some people buy horses as a business, and some people buy horses as a luxury, and you should never get the two mixed up. Everything about Pie in the Sky, from his color and his looks to his jumping ability, was pure luxury goods. And what about Onyx, right beside him? Well, that was why we had to sell him: once we knew how good he was, it would have been purest luxury to keep him. But the main reason I was walking slowly and wandering here and there was that I wanted to see Sophia. She was nowhere to be found, though.

Mom had a new haircut—with bangs! I sort of couldn't believe it, but she looked good. The bangs were pretty long, down over her eyebrows. When I said this, she said, "Two weeks and I won't be able to see a thing."

"What is Dad going to say?"

"Well, let's bet on whether he says anything. I'll give you a dollar if he says anything, and you can give me a dollar if he doesn't."

She looked young, like one of the senior girls at the high school, not the surfers, but not the science whizzes, either. I kept glancing at her as we drove home, and it did take me that long to get used to how young she was. Really, since she was only nineteen when Danny was born and twenty-four when I was born, she was probably the youngest of all my friends' mothers. And when we got home, Dad said, "Oh, you look good," but that wasn't the same thing as noticing bangs, so we called it a draw.

That night, I looked at Jane's book, and I did it the wrong way—I looked at the pictures first, and as I leafed through it, I looked at the pictures of jumping more than I looked at the pictures of hacking and riding out. There was a wonderful picture of a woman on her horse galloping through a field. Even though it was black and white, I could look at the thick grass she was galloping on and imagine how green it was. Galloping out was something we rarely did—too many gopher holes and ground squirrel holes. After I looked at the jumping pictures, I read about teaching the horses to jump, and that was fine until I came to the section called "How to Correct Jumping Defects." I read about the rushers and "apathetic galloping toward fences" without any problem. And then I got to "refusing and running out." The very first sentence read, "If you are not abusing the horse with your shifting weight, swinging legs, and hard hands, if the horse has no sore feet, if you are not asking the horse to jump higher than he knows how to, if you are not asking him to jump too much, and still your horse as a tendency to refuse (even when the approach is comfortable), then probably he is just 'chicken hearted,' and the wisest thing to do is to get rid of him." After that I read on, but I didn't really pay attention to what I was reading. I read for maybe fifteen minutes, then put the book under my bed and turned out the light. I lay there in the dark and listened to the music. It was turning out that the record player was really good for helping me not think about things that I didn't want to think about.

Truck and Horse Trailer

Lunge Line

Chapter 8

On Monday, Danny stayed for supper after we rode Blue, Oh My, and Nobby. He also helped me work Jack, and he did a funny thing: as we groomed him, Danny put his arm over Jack's back several times, at first just standing there, but then kind of leaning on him. I knew what he was doing—he was getting him ready to be ridden, but we still had not heard from Mr. Matthews, who owned the other half of him. I didn't think there was any rush, myself.

We had fried chicken, and tried to pretend that having Danny for supper was not a special occasion. The apple pie? Well, there were some apples in the store, cheap because it was fall now. All through the meal, Daddy and Danny talked about Happy, the horse Daddy had sold Danny, and who was now getting to be a good cow horse, and then about the fact that Danny had taken her to a branding. It had been pretty interesting, because they did it as slowly as possible, not as quickly. The horses were never to get out of a trot, and there was no running around for the hands—they were to approach the calves slowly and easily. Danny had liked it in some ways, but it was hard to get used to. He said, "Now, Russ Jarrow is totally opposite Jem in looks, he's got to be six-four, and he would just jog over to where the cow and the calf were and the rope would slip out of his hand and around the back end of the calf, and the calf would ease to a halt, and then just lie down, or that's what it looked like. I mean, whatever part of the calf Russ wanted to rope, the rope would go there."

"Must have taken forever."

"Well, it was slow, but it was smooth. I mean, if the guy never misses a toss, then that saves time."

Mom said, "If you drive your car at eighty all the time instead of sixty-five, you're still only going to get there a few minutes before your appointment."

Danny pretended that he didn't understand this. He said, "The other thing is that the horses are never running past where they're supposed to be, because they are completely not excited. They pay attention, though."

Daddy said, "I wouldn't mind seeing that." He pushed his plate away, and I finished my mashed potatoes and gravy. Everyone was quiet as Mom brought over the pie and the plates. I don't know why that is, but it happens every time. She said, "I found some pippins. They make the best pie, I think."

Daddy and Danny were staring at the pie like they were

going to plop their faces in it. She cut the slices and passed them around. When we had all taken our first bites, Danny sighed and said, "Well, I guess I'm going to work at the ranch where they had the branding. It's called the Marble Ranch." He said it just like it was no big deal.

Mom said, "Where is that?" and Daddy said, "What's your job?"

"About half shoeing and half looking after the cows. They have a few colts to work with, too. I guess Jake told them they might like the way I go about things. It's kind of a famous place—they have a big arena and they put on rodeos every so often, but it's really famous for the house, which is a beautiful hacienda that some rich people built in the twenties. Movie stars used to come up from Hollywood and stay. Legendary parties."

Mom and Daddy exchanged a glance.

"But they don't have those anymore. It's just trying to be a plain old cattle ranch these days."

I said, "What about Happy?"

"My guess is they like her better than they like me."

We all laughed.

"There's an apartment that goes with the job. Two rooms."

And so supper ended and I went up to my room and started my homework, but not without putting on my new album, *Sounds of Silence*. The songs were kind of sad, but that was good for doing homework. I was already thinking about how much it might cost to buy another album, but I hadn't decided which one I wanted yet. The thing to do was to get Danny to drive me somewhere, and listen to the radio the whole time.

It was when I was going into the bathroom before bed that I heard Mom and Daddy talking. The sound of their voices was coming up from the living room, and so of course I stopped and listened in to see if they were talking about me. They weren't. Mom was saying, "But I have been thinking about this for weeks. I can't get it out of my mind. I try to tell myself it's none of my business, but I don't believe myself."

"It's just a rumor."

"But she told me! It's not a rumor if her own nephew's wife said what was going on."

"Why don't we let sleeping dogs lie?"

"I tell myself that every single day."

I stood absolutely still. My main thought was that if it wasn't Mom's business, then it certainly wasn't my business, and so I had better just keep walking and not listen anymore.

A rustle of pages. Daddy opening his Bible. Well, if it was big enough for that, it was pretty big. And the other thing was that I'd never heard Mom talk in quite this tone before. Mom was the one of us who always knew what to do. I heard a sigh— it sounded like Mom. I said to myself, Time to go to bed, but I stood there anyway. Finally, Daddy read, "'And he says to them, Because of your unbelief; for verily I say unto you, If ye have faith as a grain of mustard seed, ye shall say to this mountain, Be transported hence there, and it shall transport itself; and nothing shall be impossible to you.'"

They were silent. This was a pretty familiar verse, since it was one of Daddy's favorites. Finally, Mom said, "But should I *do* anything?"

"It doesn't say to."

She said, "Okay." And then they kissed. I could hear them. I went back into my room, and came out again and stomped around a little bit.

When I thanked Sophia for letting me ride Pie in the Sky and said how nice he was, she just nodded, smiled, and said, "Colonel Hawkins thought you did a good job, and I did, too." And even though I had been planning to ask her what was wrong with Onyx and why she wasn't riding him, well, I didn't say a word. And then, all day, half the time I thought it wasn't my business, and half the time I really wanted to know. At lunchtime, I looked around our table, and wondered what each of the girls would do in my place. Stella wouldn't have cared. Gloria would have waited for Sophia to say some tiny little thing that let Gloria ask the question. Mary would have said, "So, why didn't you ride your horse?" Luisa would have passed her a note in class, since Luisa was pretty shy. Leslie would have told about something that happened at camp, like fording a rushing river, and then said how afraid she was, and waited for Sophia to chime in about being afraid to ride her horse. What was my way of doing things? Well, just to worry and mind my own business. I did try one thing, which was to sit down after lunch next to Alana, who was Sophia's old friend from her neighborhood. Sophia had introduced us, and we had talked about a couple of things, like assignments, since she was also in my biggest class, geology. I asked her if she had read the chapter about volcanoes, and she had. So then I stood around, and after a while I finally said, "You heard that I rode Pie in the Sky over the weekend."

"Sophia said you did a good job."

"So, does Sophia like Pie in the Sky, do you think?"

"Sort of. Not as much as Onyx." Then, "You wanted me to say that, right?"

"Well, if it's true."

"It's true."

"But Pie in the Sky is a wonderful horse."

"You should buy him."

I laughed—not a real laugh, but polite. Then I said, "So she really does like Onyx?"

"She rides him every day. Believe me, if she didn't like him, she would tell me. Sophia is not tactful." Then she rolled her eyes.

So even Alana didn't know that Sophia wasn't riding Onyx.

Daddy suddenly got a bee in his bonnet about Jack needing to learn about loading into a trailer. And it was true—most of our horses came to us from far away. By the time they arrived, they knew all about trailers, and even though some horses didn't enjoy the experience, they were willing to put up with it. But Jack had never left the property, so what if—

Whenever Daddy started on the what-ifs, I tried not to listen. He was right, though.

Thursday after school, I came home to find the trailer and the truck parked in the arena, Danny's truck by the barn, and Nobby, the oldest and most easygoing of the other horses, waiting to be of service.

There is really no reason why a horse should go into a trailer. Trailers are dark and small, and in the wild, a horse

would never go into a dark, small place that he had to back out of. But horses go into trailers all the time, and then they are rattled and rolled around, and they get out, and go in again. Either it is a sign that they trust us, or it is a sign of complete stupidity. I prefer to think that they trust us.

It was a pleasant day—calm and a little overcast. By the time I got home, Danny had already had Jack in the pen working off his excess energy. Nobby was in there with him now, and I could see Jack nibbling at her mane, which made her put her ears a little back, though she didn't squeal or snap at him. She walked away, and he followed her. I went and got the flag and let myself into the pen. I didn't do much with them, but I did keep Nobby walking, which meant that Jack kept following her. I thought that was good practice for following her right into the trailer. After a few minutes, Daddy called me over to the arena. I put lead ropes on both Jack and Nobby and opened the gate. Nobby, of course, waited until being told that she could follow me through the gate, and Jack found her so much more interesting than anything else that he waited, too. The three of us walked calmly over to the arena. Danny took Jack from me, and I held Nobby.

The first thing that Danny did was pretend that he was just standing there while Jack sniffed the trailer. It was the kind with a ramp that the horse was supposed to walk up, so Jack had to sniff the ramp and jump back a few times. Then he had to carefully avoid the ramp, step around it, and stretch his neck to stare into the darkness of the trailer. Then he had to sniff the fenders and the wheels and the window and even the hitch. Then he had to stare at the truck. Then he had to do all of these things on the other side. After that, he decided to ignore the trailer. At that point, Danny unsnapped the lead rope and let him go, and our job was to pay him no attention and pretend that all we cared about was Nobby. After Jack had skittered away with his tail in the air, Dad made a big deal of giving Nobby a carrot, and Nobby obliged by chewing it very loudly.

As soon as Jack came over to see what was going on, Daddy marched Nobby up the ramp into the trailer. I latched the chain across her hind end so she wouldn't back out, and Daddy went under the front bar and came out the front door.

Danny and I sat down, him on the fender of the trailer and me on the pole of one of the jumps, while Daddy made a big deal of putting some oats in a couple of buckets. When Jack came zipping over, Daddy kind of pushed him aside and walked up the ramp. He set one bucket down at the front of Jack's side of the trailer, and then he hung Nobby's bucket on her side, where she could get it. He left the front door open so that if Jack came around, he could see her eating.

Then Dad came to the back of the trailer and leaned against the side. All this time we were pretending that Jack was not staring into the trailer, that he was not putting his two front feet on the ramp and leeeaaannning forward trying to see or sniff something, that he did not give a little whinny, that he didn't sort of bounce up in frustration and trot away. Nobby rattled her bucket. It was like she had been coached on exactly what to do.

Danny was still holding the lead rope, and finally Jack went over to him and nosed his leg. Danny snapped the lead rope back on him, then just eased off the fender and started walking him. Jack went along willingly. They walked all around, and then Danny walked up the ramp and into the trailer. The lead rope had a loop in it, but Danny was watching. He wanted Jack to follow him into the trailer, at least as far as his nose, but he didn't want him to avoid the ramp and then get caught with the rope around the side of the trailer. But Jack was good. He stepped up onto the ramp and got as far as putting his front feet into the trailer. Danny gave him a bit of carrot, and asked him to back down the ramp before Jack got the idea of doing that himself.

Now it went pretty smoothly. They walked in and out several times, waited longer after going in and waited less time after going out, and sometimes Danny gave Jack the carrot and sometimes a handful of the oats. After a while, Jack was going in and backing out easy as you please, in fact looking to do it. The next thing Danny did was give Jack to me, untie Nobby in front, undo her chain, and let her back out. Now it was her turn to wander around the arena. Then he lifted the ramp and shut the door, closing up the trailer completely, and we all walked away, leaving Jack and Nobby to do whatever they wanted. They went over to the fence and started reaching for bits of grass underneath the bottom rail. We went into the house and had some water.

We went out again. Danny walked over to the trailer and let down the ramp. Now it was like Jack couldn't wait to get on there and see what was inside. We had to hold him back long enough to put the lead rope on him, and then he led Danny right in. He ate a bite of the oats, and Danny backed him out.

The second time he finished the oats, and then he had to stand there for a few minutes before Danny let him out. The third time there were no oats, and I attached the chain in the back and Danny tied him up (you never ever tie a horse before attaching the chain). Next Daddy put Nobby back in her place, and we closed up the trailer. There was a little shuffling, but I looked in the window—no panicking. Daddy got into the truck and eased it away, around the arena and out the gate. Then he stopped. Still no panic.

By suppertime, Jack seemed happy and sane in the trailer, so we put the horses out, gave them some hay, and started cleaning up. At one point, Danny said, "Ralph Carmichael taught a horse to jump today. Took him about twenty minutes."

I said, "Who's Ralph Carmichael?"

Danny said, "Do you remember Andy and Daphne, at the show? Andy was riding the Appaloosa."

"They were about the nicest people at the show."

Danny nodded. "Well, Ralph is their dad. They're staying at the Marble Ranch for a few months."

Daddy said, "How did he teach a horse to jump in twenty minutes?"

"He looped a rope around his neck and sent him around in a circle, like they do with a lunge line, but the horse was much more free somehow. Thing was, Ralph was sitting on a horse, too. His horse was trained to do everything by leg pressure. First he stood there while Ralph sent the other horse around him, about thirty feet out, then Ralph walked his horse toward a jump while the other horse was still going around, and as he stood by the jump on his horse, the other horse jumped the

jump. Never paused or hesitated. After a few times, they did it with Ralph's horse trotting, and then they went around to another jump. Andy says tomorrow they'll do it cantering." Danny shook his head. "It was like Roy Rogers or something."

I wished I'd seen it.

Danny turned to me and said, "You should see it. You should see it tomorrow. It's not far from the high school, maybe fifteen minutes. I'll pick you up at two, since Friday's the early day."

Danny had never offered to pick me up at school, so I knew I was in for something special.

As soon as I walked into the lunchroom the next day, Sophia jumped in front of me and said, "You're coming tomorrow, right?"

"I don't know. I mean, I didn't realize it was supposed to be a regular thing. I—"

"We can pay you."

I stared at her. "Why would you pay me?"

"We always pay professionals who ride our horses."

She was serious, but I barked a laugh.

"What's so funny? You get paid for teaching those girls."

"I think Jane is just being nice to me."

She said, "Maybe that's how it started. But anyway, I'm going to call you tonight, and you can ask your mom."

She was so serious and definite. I did not know how to handle Sophia. There was no telling her that I did not want to fall in love with Pie in the Sky. That would be embarrassing, and I didn't have any other real reason to refuse to ride him. Daddy and Jane surely felt that I was learning something by riding a well-trained horse. So my only hope was that Mom would say I didn't have time to stay there until noon. That wasn't much of a hope. I said, "Well, call me."

She nodded and walked away.

I truly did not understand Sophia. She was like a child, she was like a grown-up, she was like a girl, she was like a boy. She didn't seem to know that she was the only kid at the high school with serious braids to her waist, her hair parted down the middle from her forehead to the nape of her neck. She didn't seem to know that her eyes were the bluest eyes anyone had ever seen. She didn't seem to know that other kids stared at her. She didn't seem to know that she had walked away from her lunch without either eating it or throwing it in the trash can. Alana picked it up and threw it away.

What you first noticed about the Marble Ranch was the setting. You went through the gate, and there were hills covered with oaks on both sides, then a little meadow with a beautiful old oak standing there by itself, spreading and twisting in all directions, the limbs heavy but strong, the leaves just floating in the light. Right when you noticed that, the hill fell away into a wide valley that rolled back, golden and soft, to layers of retreating hills. The field to the left of the road was fenced, and Hereford cattle were grazing peacefully. To the right of the road was a big pond full of ducks and other birds, and behind that was a huge arena with two cattle chutes, one at the near end and one at the far end, and a small red equipment building. A bay horse was standing in the arena, his head over the

there, moving poles and jump standards. If I hadn't known he was their father, I would have thought he was their grandfather—he had white hair sort of fluffing around his face, and also a white mustache that had been smoothed into bars with the ends turned up. He was tall and wiry—Andy came to about his chin. "Ready?" said Mr. Carmichael, then to us, "Nice and quiet here now. Beautiful spot at this time of day."

Andy took Barry Boy over to one corner and began lunging him while Ralph set three jumps down the center of the pen. If you drew a line, one would be on one side of the line, a single vertical, and on the other side, an in-and-out. Opposite to the vertical, along the rail of the pen, he set up another vertical. I saw right away what they were going to do—if you lunged the horse in a circle on one side of the pen, you could jump him over the in-and-out, and if you lunged him on the other side of the pen, the two verticals would be on opposite sides of the lunging circle.

Andy was hopping around in the middle of the circle, waving his arms, then springing suddenly at Barry Boy, even saying, "Boo!" Barry Boy flinched once, and kicked up his heels once, and I saw that the Carmichaels viewed lunging the way I saw working the round corral—not a way for the horse to learn to settle down, but a way to get the bucks out. When Ralph and Daphne had set the jumps the way they wanted, Andy took off Barry Boy's halter and walked away from the horse at a brisk clip. Barry Boy trotted after him. When Barry Boy got to Andy, Ralph called out, "Yup!" and Andy gave Barry Boy a treat of some sort.

Then Barry Boy had to move around the whole pen. He

didn't always canter and he didn't always trot, but he had to do something, and at a good pace. Ralph wanted him active and loose and free. He ran past the jumps, ran around the periphery, bucked and played. I would not say we chased him, but we encouraged him, or maybe we played with him, and after a while, he turned toward Ralph, who was standing near one of the railings, and he cantered toward him, and happened to jump one of the fences. Immediately, Ralph called out, "Yup!" and Barry Boy went to him and received a lump of sugar. Now we went back to playing. A couple of minutes later, Barry Boy jumped again, this time the jump that had been set up along the rail, and Ralph shouted, "Yup!" and Daphne handed out the sugar. All the Carmichaels were equipped with sugar. Barry Boy proceeded to put two and two together—he turned and voluntarily jumped the center vertical and then went straight to Ralph as soon as Ralph called out, "Yup!"

Danny said, "He never forgets the 'yup,' because that's the signal to the horse that he is going to get the sugar lump."

Then Daphne put Barry Boy's halter back on him and led him to one side of the in-and-out while Ralph went to the other side. When Daphne unhooked the lead rope, Ralph shouted, "Yup!" and Barry Boy cantered to him—three strides to the fence, then over, then a stride in between, then over, then two strides to Ralph, then a lump of sugar.

I said to Danny, "Why doesn't he go around the jumps?"

Danny said, "Because a straight line is the shortest distance between two points, or between him and his reward."

"But why make the effort to jump?"

"Because for Barry Boy, it isn't an effort, it's a pleasure."

Next, they put him on the lunge line and they lunged him over the fences, first the two single verticals and then the in-and-out. They let him do it his own way and find his own pace, which was easy and graceful, as if he knew exactly how to get himself around the circle and over the fences.

I said to Danny, "How many times has he done this?"

"Oh, this is the fourth time, maybe."

And he did it willingly—he got so into the rhythm that he kept jumping the two fences on the circle until they had to ask him to stop in order to raise the fences. I said, "Blue needs to do this."

Danny said, "That's what I thought. And you know what?"

"What?"

"If he saw a couple of other horses having fun doing it, he might think that it could be fun, too."

"Do they do this with all the horses?"

"Oh, they do all sorts of things. Usually, they have three or more in the ring together. There's one here, a filly, who just loves to jump. Two days ago, they had her in here with two of the others, and she was jumping all the fences—just turning to them and going over them, and then the three of them were loping around the arena, and she turned and jumped right out. That's four and a half feet. It was like she looked at the jumps and she looked at the fence, and she said to herself, 'What's the difference?' And when she was out, she didn't even run back to the barn—she just trotted along the fence and Andy let her in the gate."

After that, the Carmichaels put the saddle and bridle on Barry Boy, and Andy got on him, and they did the same things with Andy in the saddle that Barry Boy had done on his own. Sometimes Ralph rewarded him and sometimes he didn't, but if he was going to, he always exclaimed, "Yup!" Andy was a good rider—firm seat, but easy and light with his legs and his hands. He made his part seem like just joining in the game, too.

They stopped. The session hadn't gone on for more than half an hour, if that, and then Andy took Barry Boy up along the hillside for at least that long. Ralph sniffed and then said, maybe to us, "You want a jumper, well, you got to make jumping the fun part. When we've got cattle to work, we jump first and go out and do our daily business after." Then he said, "Most any horse can jump, and a fair number of them think jumping is the most fun. It's like these racehorses. You aren't going to make a great racehorse out of a horse who doesn't love to run, and not all of them do. I had a friend down at Santa Anita—he had a horse with talent to burn, but he was a sulky one, and even though he won a stakes or two, my friend just never got an honest race out of him, because the horse had no vocation for it. But if jumping is always fun, then even the ones who don't love it can enjoy it."

It was now getting toward evening—the sky above the mountains was heading toward blue-gray, and the air was cooling fast. Danny and I walked back to the car. Daphne came with us, carrying her tack, Ralph stayed in the pen, moving things around, and Andy rode Barry Boy up the hill on a loose rein. I couldn't stop glancing at Daphne—she was as cheerful and as strong as any girl I had ever met. But I didn't ask any questions. The Carmichaels were way too mysterious for that.

Water Trough

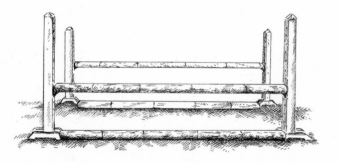

In and Out Jump

Chapter 9

IT WAS NOT SOPHIA WHO CALLED THAT NIGHT, IT WAS JANE. And Mom answered the phone, because I was upstairs doing homework and listening to music. I didn't even hear it ring. Since I hadn't said a word to Mom about Pie in the Sky except "fine," when she came upstairs and told me about it, she was all happy and excited. She sort of bounced into my room, and said, "Oh, that was Jane. She said that you are doing so well on Pie in the Sky that they want you to keep riding him. I don't see how you can do that during the week, but maybe something will work out. Jane says that this is a big opportunity for you—Colonel Hawkins is so impressed by your riding, and he is not easy to impress! You should be proud, sweetie!"

I nodded. Then I said, "But I don't have time to ride our horses. And it's getting dark earlier."

"Well, I can help. I mean, your dad and I think you should be open to opportunities, and according to Jane, riding this horse is an opportunity."

"I like him—"

"I can ride Morning Glory and Nobby."

I looked at her and said, "You can ride Blue if Dad is with you. Barbie rode him a lot. He likes to take care of his rider."

"I've been looking at him very fondly."

I shrugged.

"That would make time for you at least a couple of afternoons a week."

"Did she say anything about them paying me?"

"Oh, goodness, Abby, no. I wouldn't ask—"

"I'm not asking. But Sophia said something about that today, and it gives me the creeps, so if they say anything about that, just tell them I'll do it for free."

"Of course!"

We exchanged a look that said that this part was something we would not tell Dad.

After Mom left, I sat there gazing out the window at the gelding pasture. It was dark, and there wasn't much of a moon, but I could see Lincoln and Blue standing by themselves. Probably they were under the trees wondering where the pest, Jack, had gotten to. Daddy was talking about going back to Oklahoma and buying a few horses, but he couldn't decide whether to wait until he sold a couple of the mares, so that he could spend a little more money, or whether to go now and have a look before it got terribly cold. Mom had been serving a lot of beans lately, so I knew it was time to sell something. Oh My would be the one—she would go for good money, since she was safe and beautiful, with unusual markings. But the best time to sell a fancy horse is the early spring, when the showing and rodeo season is about to begin, and people feel good that they got through the winter and are ready to spend a little in order to show off—and Oh My was a show-off horse if ever there was one. The ideal thing would be to take her to a roundup or a rodeo and just walk around—paint-horse lovers would be running up to Dad and asking if they could write a check. But that was six months away.

And then there was Blue. I had made up my mind that he was a really good horse—it was all in his canter. It was so floating and easy that I thought that one thing would make up for everything else about him, but even though we'd had him for six months now, we didn't know what else he had. Because he was a grown-up horse and his previous owner or owners had never asked him to do much, we had spent the time since my broken arm healed just teaching him things he should have already known—how to respond to the aids, how to move his feet, how to turn handily and go readily about his job. He had learned how to not be afraid—in that he was like Pie in the Sky. But since they had started Pie in the Sky doing his job as a young horse, the thing Pie in the Sky knew first was doing his job, and the thing he knew second was being afraid. Once he cleared away the fear, his job was easy. Blue had learned to be afraid first and to do his job second. Once he cleared away the fear, he still had to make an effort to do his job. Maybe that was the reason Peter Finneran and the whip didn't make Blue better—the whip just added fear to fear, and covered up his job even more.

I loved Blue. But maybe my love for him would not have a happy ending.

Up until Jack was born, Daddy had insisted on lots of things, and one of them was that we not name the horses special names. I always hated that, because I lost track of the horses who came and went, and even the most special ones got hazy in my mind. Without names, who was the one who bucked me off, who was the one who lay down next to me in the pasture when I was sick, who was the one who liked peanut butter and jelly sandwiches, who was the one who could rear on command (not a skill Daddy had known about when he bought her, or he wouldn't have bought her), who was the one who kicked down sixty feet of fence? I didn't know. They came and they went, though the stories stuck around, always beginning with "Who was the one who . . . ?"

But when they had names, I remembered everything about them. Lester was the one Daddy loved the most. Sapphire was the one who licked me all over like a foal once when I was upset, Amazon was totally responsible and bossy, Jack was the one who was just too amazing to be named like all the others, and Blue, True Blue, was the kind and faithful one, the best friend, the one who, if I trained him properly, would be able to do anything. I saw maybe for the first time that Daddy's way of not naming the horses was there for a reason. I sighed.

The record ended, and there was a moment of the *huff huff* of the needle getting to the center, then I could hear the arm lift and move back to its resting place, and then it was quiet. A horse whinnied—one of the mares, since it was coming from the other side of the house. I wondered what Jack was doing. Just then, I saw him—he came galloping and kicking out of the trees, then went to the watering trough and took a drink. After that he tossed his head, playing in the water until he was plenty wet. I smiled. What he was doing was being himself.

Ellen showed up first, and then Melinda's lesson was a little short because she didn't feel well, so I got to the barn early, handed Gallant Man to Rodney, and headed for the bathroom. When I came out of the bathroom, I saw Sophia and her dad, or it must have been her dad, because he was old and blond and had his arm around her shoulders. Sophia said something, and he laughed. When he laughed, he threw his head back and I got a good look at him. He looked like a movie star.

Just then, Rodney brought out Pie in the Sky and handed the reins to Sophia, who took them. I walked toward them. Mr. Rosebury turned and saw me coming. He said, "Oh, here you are, Abigail. I've been wanting to meet you." He held out his hand.

I shook it and said, "You can call me Abby. They only call me Abigail when I'm in trouble."

"Ah," said Mr. Rosebury. "That's when they call me Henderson J. Rosebury the third, so I understand what you're getting at."

Sophia handed me Pie in the Sky's reins. She had not yet smiled at me, but she didn't seem mad. She just seemed like Sophia. Colonel Hawkins came out of the stall and down the aisle with Onyx, and Jane appeared from her office. The colonel and I mounted our horses and headed for the big arena. Jane and Sophia walked together, and Mr. Rosebury walked along beside Colonel Hawkins, talking. I could hear him pretty well.

"What a pair of winners we've got now, right, Colonel? I am really looking forward to next year. I know we've done well this year—I mean, six championship ribbons is nothing to sneeze at—but why not a perfect season? These guys ought to be winning everything. They're young, they're sound, they're—"

"Now, Joe," said Colonel Hawkins. "How many times do I have to tell you these are horses? If you owned a baseball team, would you always be looking for the perfect game?"

"Sure! Why not? If you don't look for it, you aren't going to find it." He laughed. He must have sensed me looking at him, because he turned and smiled. He seemed like a happy person. He had Sophia's blue eyes. I smiled, because if you don't smile when grown-ups are smiling at you, they think you're being sassy.

In the arena, Mr. Rosebury followed Sophia to the center and stood between her and Jane. He kept talking, but I couldn't hear him because the colonel and I were starting to warm up Onyx and Pie in the Sky.

It was only then that I realized that Pie in the Sky wasn't ready to work. All the time we were walking over he'd been hesitating and dancing, and I hadn't done a thing about it because I was paying attention to Mr. Rosebury. Now, in the arena, Pie in the Sky gave a little hop and a snort, and when I asked him to back up, he just stood there, and after a couple of seconds, he started telling me with his stiff neck and back that he just might start bucking if I didn't watch out. Rally Rally Rally was what this said to me. Pie in the Sky was a chestnut, like Rally, or, as we originally called him, Ornery George, and just glancing down at his red-gold coat gave me, first, the sense that something was about to go wrong and, second, the memory of Jem Jarrow telling me never to be too lazy to dismount. I dismounted and led Pie in the Sky over to the corner of the arena and used his reins to work him a little in both directions, getting him to step over and bend his back.

I had no idea if he'd done this sort of lesson with anyone other than Danny, but he was a talented and athletic horse, and he did exactly as I asked. After twice to the right and twice to the left, I asked him to step back, and he still hesitated, so I did it twice to the right again and once to the left. After that, he backed up and lowered his head, and just for good measure, I asked him to bend his neck and touch his side with his nose.

Just then, Mr. Rosebury said, "What are you doing with my horse, Abigail?"

I jumped. He was right beside me, and I hadn't seen him coming. I said, "I'm getting him to loosen his back."

"It's quite odd-looking, what you're doing."

"I'm doing it so he won't buck me off."

He retreated a step, and said, "Never seen that before. Horse looks a little bothered."

I said, "I'd rather have him bothered with me on the ground than with me riding him. Sir."

I was glad they weren't paying me, because that meant I

didn't have to do it their way. I glanced over at Sophia. She was staring at us. I said, "He seems looser now." I walked Pie in the Sky to the fence and mounted.

He was looser, but he wasn't really loose. Time to hope for the best.

We trotted and cantered around, doing circles and figure eights. I tried with each turn to lift Pie in the Sky's shoulder and move him a little to the outside, just to bend him in both directions. Colonel Hawkins liked a preliminary hand gallop, and that was good, though Pie in the Sky did give one little buck in the corner. Bucks are good when the horse is on his own, not so good when you are riding him. On his own, he is just getting stuff out of his system. When you are on him, he might start by getting stuff out of his system and go on to thinking that he would like to toss you off his back. I was still hoping for the best.

Onyx, of course, was completely relaxed, as always, so Colonel Hawkins finished his hand gallop by turning in a big circle and heading down over one of the smaller verticals and then looping out in the other direction to another fence, a small oxer. Now everyone looked at me, expecting me to follow him, but I didn't think Pie in the Sky was ready, so I just came down to the trot and made a few more circles.

Jane pointed me toward a triple in-and-out, small and easy, the fences graduated from about 2'6" to about 3 feet. The heights should have been no trouble for Pie in the Sky, but he almost refused the first one, and I had to kick him to get him over the second one and the third one. And here is where I learned something about both Pie in the Sky and Blue. I learned that when Pie in the Sky tried to refuse, he was testing me to see if I was in charge, and when Blue refused, he really was just scared.

Quite often a horse will behave himself the first time you ride him, being a good boy because he doesn't know you. A ride or two later—Daddy called it the "second ride rule," but it can happen on the third ride or the fourth—he thinks he does know you, and so some horses try to push you, to see what they can get away with. I knew with all my heart that Pie in the Sky was doing this. He was not afraid—I didn't sense in his body any ripple of nervous energy. His ears pricked, but they didn't arrow forward in worry. I was sure that if I'd been able to see his face, I would have seen a grumpy look, so once we got over the last fence, I trotted to Jane and said, "Got a whip? I forgot to bring one."

She went to the gate and picked up one of the two or three that were lying under the fence. She handed it to me. I took it lash down, but I did flick it outward once, so Pie in the Sky would know that I knew that he knew I had it. We trotted a circle and picked up the canter and went back toward the fence. He slowed down about three strides out, and I flicked the whip again. He jumped, but not smoothly. So I did not go down over the other two jumps—I turned out, went back, and came again. This time, I smacked him on the haunches about six strides out, at the same time keeping steady hold of the reins. He tucked his haunches, focused on the jumps, and went down through them perfectly. That is another thing about a horse who is testing you—most of the time, they accept being punished.

The test was over, and the rest of the lesson was fun. The last course was eight fences, 3'9", a little twisty. The first time through, Pie in the Sky was about 20 percent disorganized, but just like the week before, he seemed to use that trip to learn the path on his own, because the second time through, he was like a machine. As before, his feet seemed attached by rubber bands to my head. Every time I turned to look at the next fence, his body curved and his feet went there. Once again, it was an uncanny feeling. Mr. Rosebury came over and slapped me on the leg, the way some people slap each other on the back when they are happy, and he said, "Great go, Abby! Just perfect."

I walked Pie in the Sky away from him, cooling the horse out, and said, "Thank you, Mr. Rosebury. He's a really good horse." But he stayed alongside me, still talking. "Well, you know, he came from Calvin Murphy down in LA—you know him? He's a character. Sometimes he takes forty horses to a show, eight girls riding them. They sweep the ribbons. He doesn't ride anymore himself, I guess—he had an accident, not even a horse accident but a motorcycle accident—but he's got these girls like a team or a platoon of soldiers. They ride eight, nine horses a day, and he's got a system, and the horses learn. Pie in the Sky, he told me himself, was one of his best, and I bought him without Sophy even trying him, I just liked him so much. Well, I learned my lesson there, let me tell you. But there's something in that horse, some real star power, so I don't let her give up on him. I say, 'You know, he's just going to hang around, Soph, until you make up your mind to do the deed.'"

When we got back to the barn and Rodney had taken

Onyx, the colonel came over and said, "Thanks, Abby," and led both Pie in the Sky and Mr. Rosebury away.

When Sophia and Jane arrived, Jane was saying, "There's no rush, but, Sophia, you don't want to let your skills fade. Are you listening to me? I don't have the sense that you are. A month or two, well, but . . ." She waved to me as I trotted to the parking lot.

When we got home, there was another letter from Barbie, and another drawing, this one of Alexis telling the other kids at the Jackson School what to do—Barbie drew Alexis with her arm in the air and her mouth open, and six girls and guys making beds, washing dishes, scrubbing the floor, and weeding the flower beds; a teacher was looking on, scratching his head. Barbie drew herself off in the background, sitting on her horse and smiling. There wasn't much to the written part of the letter, but in this case the picture really was worth a thousand words. I tacked it up next to the earlier envelopes.

On Monday our ancient history teacher was sick and they hadn't been able to find a substitute, so they had Mr. Reynolds give us a study hall, and he was strict—no talking. I read our English book. We had finished *The Red Badge of Courage* and were on to *Animal Farm*, in which the pigs were the bosses and the horses just did as they were told. It was not like any farm I had ever seen, but the book was fun to read. I could tell by looking at Sophia that she really wanted to talk to me, but with Mr. Reynolds there was no chance even of passing a note.

Finally, at lunchtime, I was carrying my tray past where Sophia and Alana were sitting to my usual table, and when I stopped next to Sophia and began, "That was gr—" she reached up, grabbed my arm, and said, "Abby! Sit down."

I could see Gloria and Leslie watching us. "I've got to—"

"No, really. Sit down. I have an idea." She kept holding my arm, and my tray began to tilt. I looked at Alana, who was staring off toward the windows. My tray tilted a little more, and the plate slid toward the edge. I sat down.

"Okay," said Sophia. "This is what we're going to do. When the show season starts, you are going to ride Pie in the Sky in all the shows. Around here, but also down in LA. My dad wants to go to all of them and then sell Pie in the Sky for a lot of money. Jane thinks it's a good idea." Her eyes were incredibly wide open and her face was even paler than usual.

I said, "That would be fun, Sophia, but I have—"

Her voice got louder. "We would pay you. My dad would call up your dad and talk him into it. He can talk anyone into anything. I mean, he talks. Money talks. They both talk."

I laughed, and then I sat down next to Sophia and looked her in the eye. "Look, Sophia," I started, whispering because of Alana. "You should be riding your horse, at least Black G— I mean, Onyx. I like Pie in the Sky, but he's too . . ." I sighed. "I have horses of my own. I have to ride them."

All of a sudden, Sophia put her head down on the table. Alana looked surprised. She said, "Soph! What are you doing?"

Then Sophia groaned and fell out of her chair onto the floor. Her chair fell over, too. The lunchroom went quiet, and everyone started looking at us. Gloria stood up, but the first person to come over was one of the tennis coaches. She knelt beside Sophia and put her hand across her forehead, like maybe she had a fever, and said, "What happened? My goodness!"

Within about a minute of that, teachers and the assistant principal were pushing us out of the way, and then the nurse was there, and she said, "Oh, I think she just fainted. She'll come around." She pushed some chairs back and let her lie stretched out. The tennis coach stood the chair up again. I took my tray over to our usual table, and Stella said in a loud voice, "What in the world was that all about?" The others wanted to know, too, but I just shrugged.

As soon as they carried Sophia off to the nurse's office, Miss Helmich, the assistant principal, motioned Alana and me over to where she was standing and said, "You girls come with me. I'll give you notes for your teachers."

It felt like we were in the police station or something. Miss Helmich wrote everything we said on a pad, and kept nodding and asking more questions. I let Alana do most of the talking. Yes, she and Sophia had come to school together that morning. Alana's mother had driven them. Sophia had seemed fine; she hadn't complained of any kind of dizziness, headache, or stomachache. She hadn't said how much sleep she had gotten the night before. She'd carried her books into school. She'd been the same as she always was.

"How about you, Abby? Did you notice anything different about her? Was she pale, for example?"

I said, "Sophia is always pale."

"Nothing struck you?"

I said, "Well, when I was walking by, I noticed that she hadn't eaten anything on her plate."

"Alana?"

"She said she didn't like the meatloaf."

"Carrots? Bread? Anything?"

Alana shook her head.

"What does she eat for breakfast?"

"Some toast, I guess. I mean, I don't go over there for breakfast. But she's not a big eater anyway. If she doesn't like it, she doesn't eat it. Once when we were in like third grade, her mom made her sit at the table until she tasted something, I can't remember what it was. She sat at the table until three in the morning."

"Is that possible?" said Miss Helmich.

I said, "Yes."

Miss Helmich said, "Has she been getting thinner?"

Alana said, "I don't know. She's really modest. She doesn't even go in her family's swimming pool. I wouldn't be able to tell."

Miss Helmich looked at me. I said, "I only see her in riding clothes, with long sleeves and usually a jacket. Where we ride it's mostly chilly, so I wear a jacket, too."

"This isn't good," said Miss Helmich.

Then Alana said, "Miss Helmich, you should talk to my mom. She thinks Sophia is a real oddball, but she never says that to Sophia's mom or anything like that. But every time I ask her if she wants to do something, even just go to a movie or to the mall to go shopping, she says no. And she hasn't made any friends. The only people she talks to are me and Abby."

Miss Helmich lowered her voice. "Does she attempt to prevent you from making friends, Alana?"

Alana scooted around in her chair, then said, "Well, she made me promise to always sit with her at lunch, but I have other friends that I sit with in classes and gym. I've made friends."

Miss Helmich drummed her fingers on the desk and took a deep breath. A moment later the nurse came to the door. We could see her through the little glass windowpane. She waved her hand; Miss Helmich excused herself and went out into the hall for a minute.

I said, "Alana, do you know that Sophia hasn't been riding her horses?"

Alana shook her head. She looked pretty miserable. After a moment, she said, "Sophia and I were real friends in fourth grade, and I guess third grade. I mean, we live next door to each other, and so my mom keeps thinking that it's just like it used to be, but I am allergic to dogs and I hate horses, so what do we have to talk about?"

"I don't know." Then I said, "TV?"

Alana smiled, but I hadn't realized that I was being funny. The things Stella, Gloria, and I talked about were mostly TV and magazines, which I saw when I went to Gloria's. Or music. At lunch we talked about the other kids or the teachers. Or homework, but only to say how boring it was; I supposed Kyle Gonzalez could have talked about how interesting homework was, but he didn't have anyone to talk to. Everyone at school had plenty of things he or she would not dare to talk about with anyone or, maybe, only with one other person. I had them, too.

Miss Helmich came back in, and I saw the nurse go away. Miss Helmich said, "Well, she seems okay. She told Mrs. Beach that she had missed breakfast. I called her mother."

She wrote on a little pad, then handed us each a note. That was the last we saw of Sophia for that week.

On Saturday, we got to the stable in time for me to go with Melinda from the parking lot to the barn. I asked her if she was feeling better.

She said, "Oh, I am. There is something going around. Every time there is something going around, I get it. Last year, when I was living in LA, I got ringworm. Did you ever have that? I had to wear this cloth helmet over my head for such a long time. Mom would not let them shave my head, though. You cannot scratch even though it itches like crazy. This boy in my class had to shave his head."

"No, I don't think so."

"Well, you would know if you got it. Maybe I got it at the hairdresser. That's what Nanny thought."

Rodney hoisted her on Gallant Man while she was still talking. We had a much more serious lesson than we had had the previous week—lots of cantering and jumping, though not very high, and Melinda did a good job. She almost never said anything about being scared anymore, and she always patted her pony after every exercise. Afterward, she dismounted by herself and led Gallant Man around while we waited for Ellen. Then, once I had given Ellen a leg up while Melinda held the pony, Melinda took a sugar cube out of her pocket. When she was sure Ellen was watching, she gave it to him. She got the reaction she was after—Ellen's eyebrows dipped down and she sniffed. But Melinda just smiled, waved, and said, "See you next week!"

Jane came into the ring while I was teaching Ellen, and she stood there for a few minutes, watching and nodding. Ellen immediately stuck her chin out a bit too much, because she loved an audience, no matter how small. Finally, Jane came over to me and said, "So what's your version of what happened to Sophia at school?"

"She fainted and fell out of her chair, and they took her to the nurse's office, and that's the last I saw her. I guess she wasn't eating anything. At least, I never saw her eat anything at school."

"Her mother says it was a mistake to send her to a public school. Too big and impersonal."

"What does that mean?"

"You know, with such large classes, some kids get lost in the crowd."

"Isn't that a good thing?"

Jane laughed, and I shouted to Ellen to trot a nice figure eight, making sure that her circles were round. She did it as if she had been using a compass. I shouted, "Pat your pony, then do it again at the canter, changing leads through the trot. Rouunndd." She needed two tries for that.

Jane said, "Do you think the Peter Finneran clinic had anything to do with this?"

I said, "He was very mean."

"Well, he was strict."

I called to Ellen, "Now you are going to do your serpentine. Start at that end, and make three loops around the jumps and end at that end." I pointed. Ellen was careful to make her loops even. Probably when she did her homework, she never ever forgot to put her name on it, along with her address, and the mark she expected to receive—even though she was only in third grade.

Then I said to Jane, "I thought he was a bully. Especially to

167

Sophia. When she got mad and walked out, I heard him say, 'One down, four to go.'"

"Oh, he talks like that. Very . . . I don't know, extravagant. Don't you know anyone who talks sort of like he's singing a song? Showing off, in a way."

"Was he being funny?"

Jane said, "Maybe he thought so."

"Well, we didn't. He made me want to cry, too, but I was so mad I decided he would never make me cry."

"Who was crying?"

"Sophia."

"She was? I've never seen Sophia cry. Even when she fell off about two years ago and really quite smashed her shoulder, she didn't shed a tear."

"Well, she cried."

I went over to the four cavalletti and turned them so that they were middle height, then I counted steps between them so that they would be the right distance for the pony. Ellen went around with a happy look on her face and trotted over them. The pony was as neat as you please, and Ellen said, "That was good!"

Jane came over and said to me, "What did he say to you?"

"He called Blue a worthless beast."

"That's just an expression."

I said, "I didn't realize that." Even the thought was making me a little mad. I waved Ellen over the cavalletti again, but I hardly had to—she was already coming. As she passed me, she said, "Put them up!"

I flipped them up and spread them, so the pony would have to canter. It was a nice exercise, and one that I enjoyed, that bouncing through the cavalletti at a nice springy pace. Behind me, Jane was walking around in a little circle. When she came over, I said, "Well, we paid him plenty of money, and he acted like he was doing us a favor even talking to us or watching us. I did think he was mean. If that's just the way he talks, then maybe you should have told us ahead of time."

Ellen went through the cavalletti twice, grinning each time, her hands firmly on the pony's neck, the way I had taught her, and her heels down. Then she came back the other way.

Jane said, "Come to my office when you're finished, and we can chat about this."

I nodded.

After she left, I set up four jumps in a row, not very high, sort of like big cavalletti, only farther apart, and I had her canter down over them on a pretty loose rein. She was excited. I put them up one hole. She did fine. I decided not to push my—her—luck. When we got back to the barn, she told Rodney that she was getting "really good."

Rodney said, "I'm sure y'are, lass. I've got great hopes for ya."

Ellen kissed him on the cheek.

Jane was eating a muffin at her desk and drinking a cup of coffee. She wiped her mouth when I came in, and said, "Well, Abby. Hmm. Say one more thing about Peter Finneran."

I said, "He doesn't make it fun."

Jane looked out the window. I think she was talking to herself without saying anything. Finally, she turned, took another bite of her muffin, and said, "What he wants to do is toughen you girls up. He wants you to get angry and decide to do better."

"What if we get angry and are mean to our horses?"

169

"I think he would stop you."

I said, and I knew this was sassy, "And if Blue were his horse, he would just keep whipping him until Blue did what he wanted?"

"Well, no. Of course he would recognize that Blue is a sensitive animal—"

"Maybe Sophia is sensitive, too."

Jane said, "Maybe she is. But, Abby, Peter Finneran's job isn't the same as my job or, say, your friend Jem's job. Our job is to find a way to bring every horse and every child along, if that's possible. His job is to cull the herd."

"What does that mean?"

"That means, part of what he does when he goes around giving clinics is look for horses and riders that might go really far, like get on the team. That is only a handful of riders. They have to be talented and experienced, but they also have to have a certain temperament. Do you know what that is?"

I nodded. "You mean, just the way that they are, starting when they're born."

"Yes."

"Like my colt Jack is bold and full of energy."

"Yes."

"So what is Sophia's temperament?"

Jane stared at me. I hoped that she wasn't going to do what the teachers at school liked to do, which was to say, "What do *you* think?" But she was nicer than that. She said, "I thought Sophia was tough as nails. So did Colonel Hawkins. That time she hurt her shoulder, she almost had him convinced to let her keep riding."

I said, "Has he asked her why she doesn't want to ride her horses?"

"I don't know. I don't know that the colonel ever asks why."

"Why not?"

"Well, you know. 'Theirs not to reason why, Theirs but to do and die.'"

"What does that mean?"

"Oh, it's a poem, 'The Charge of the Light Brigade.' It's about being in the cavalry, which Colonel Hawkins was in for years before it disbanded."

"Well, someone should ask her."

"Someone should," said Jane.

When I was walking out to the parking lot to wait for Mom, I went by Pie in the Sky's stall and spoke to him. He looked at me, but he didn't come over for a pat. Onyx, though, came right to his stall door, put his head over, and nickered at me. He was still my friend.

Bridle Without Reins

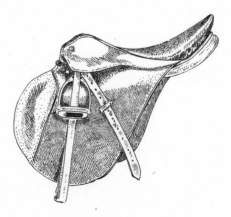

English Saddle

Chapter 10

THAT AFTERNOON, WHEN I WAS WORKING WITH BLUE, I thought about what Jane had said. I hadn't told her everything that was in my mind, but partly that was because the things that were in my mind weren't very clear even to me. While I brushed Blue and he did his usual thing of knowing exactly where I was and staying out of my way, and also cooperating and being a good boy, I wondered about Sophia and Pie in the Sky. Pie in the Sky had a temperament just like Blue or Jack or Onyx did, and I had experienced it enough for it to be pretty vivid in my mind. In some ways, he was most like Jack—he had what I would have to call pride. He wanted to do things his way and he felt his way was right, but his way wasn't always right. It was like he was saying all the time, "I know what I'm doing," even if he didn't really. Onyx did know what he was doing, so he just did it, and it was easy to go along with him. Onyx had not pride but self-confidence. It was not easy to offend Onyx, but it was easy to offend Pie in the Sky, and if you offended him, he got back at you by refusing or bucking. People talk a lot about pride. If I'd asked Dad, he could have reeled off ten quotes from the Bible about pride. The one we always talked about in church was "Pride goes before destruction, a haughty spirit before a fall." I knew that one by heart.

When I was brushing Blue's face with the soft brush, I said, "You don't have a haughty spirit, do you? No. You are a sweetheart."

Obviously, Sophia had lots of pride. That was the reason she pretended not to notice any of the other kids, and that was the reason she did things her way, like the braids. And probably that was the reason she rode the way she did—her position was always correct and she never forgot what she was doing. If she was supposed to make a fifteen-foot circle and then go down over the two jumps with three strides in between, that's what she did. And if she was scared of anything (how high the jump was, how big the water was, or how tight the turn was), her pride meant that she wouldn't ever let on.

I put the English saddle on Blue—the nice brown one that his owner had bought for him—and then his English bridle, and I led him to the mounting block. I still didn't know what we were going to do, but once I was sitting in the saddle, I decided to try riding him on a loose rein, the way Mr. Littauer recommended in the book Jane had loaned me. It seemed like an experiment, but as I was doing it, I realized that not much was different from my normal way of riding him—of course I let him go on a loose rein when we were finished with an exercise or at the end of a ride. What was different was how I felt about it. At the end of a ride, I would be relaxing and thinking about what we had been doing or about what was coming. But now, at the beginning of the ride, I was not relaxing. Mr. Littauer said that a horse on a loose rein with his head down is a relaxed and happy horse, more like a horse on his own in the pasture. We made bigger and bigger circles, and pretty soon we began to trot. What I noticed was that Blue did act like a horse in the pasture—he glanced here and there, and his ears flicked around. He went where I told him to go, but his attention wasn't completely on me. Was this good or bad? We kept going.

I was surprised at how uncomfortable my experiment made me feel. I really wanted to pick up the reins, at least a little. But Mr. Littauer said that picking up the reins raises the horse's energy level, and you want the horse's energy level to stay low. It was also hard to lean forward the way that the lady in the pictures was doing—not physically hard, of course, but mentally hard, because what if he stumbled? What if he put his head down? These were things I never normally thought about. But Mr. Littauer said that if you were balanced over the horse's center of gravity and going along with him, he would be less likely to stumble. He would just carry himself and you in the easiest possible way. I made myself find that spot, that moving spot, where he and I were exactly together.

Then we cantered. I put my heels way down, like the lady in the picture, and made my back very straight, so my shoulders did look sort of soldiery. I made my elbows and hands as loose as I could, and though the reins weren't flapping, they were loose. I did not feel Blue's mouth. Blue seemed to stretch a little bit, and lift his front end. As far as I could tell from the saddle, his head was up and his nose was out, just like the horse in the picture. And if I'd thought his canter was delightful before, well, doing it this way was amazing. It really was like flying along. Blue seemed to enjoy himself, too. We went around the arena three or four times in each direction. When we were finished, Blue was hardly sweating. Afterward, I didn't know what I thought about it, except that it surprised me that being relaxed could be so scary. But it was fun, too. There is something pretty irresistible about an activity that is both scary and enjoyable. I patted Blue on the neck and asked him to walk. I picked up the reins enough to hold them, but not enough to make contact. We wandered toward the arena. Nobby whinnied to us, and Blue looked at her but kept walking.

So if your horse was prideful, like Pie in the Sky, maybe that was why he was willing to jump those big jumps—not for fun, like Onyx, but for showing off. I knew from riding Pie in the Sky, though, that when his pride was offended, you had to persuade him to cooperate by convincing him that you knew what you were doing. That meant that you had to get him to jump the course your way by keeping your leg on, flicking the whip, and knowing where you were going. If you did that, then the next time around the course, he did it your way, but even better—he showed off doing it your way.

Really, though, I didn't want to think anymore about Pie in the Sky—not my horse, never to be my horse. I wanted to try that loose-reins thing again. I made myself not pick up the reins, and tried to guide Blue with my weight and my legs. He understood. We made some big loops in both directions at the walk. I patted him, then urged him up to the trot. He was lively about it. He seemed to understand what we were doing better than he had the first time, so he moved more willingly and supplely. I made tighter loops and circles, using only my weight and legs. With each turn, he got better at it. I forced myself not to think what if, or to remember those big spooks I had seen him do when we first got him. We just went around, and if I wasn't quite relaxed, well, he seemed to be.

Finally, I did pick up a rein—the right one, but very lightly—I just used it to ask him to bend his body a little bit as he went through the turn, then I dropped it.

I wondered about Peter Finneran. Maybe he had seen how much pride Sophia had, and decided to do something about it, and maybe he had succeeded. Maybe Sophia had stopped riding her horses because she wasn't proud of her riding anymore after the way he talked to her and about her in front of us. And then I thought, What business was it of his? But it did seem to fit what the proverb said—Sophia's pride had gone before her destruction, and her haughty spirit had led to a fall (even if it wasn't an actual fall from her horse).

I got Blue to turn to the left, using just a little rein again, and then dropping it. Now the interesting part—stopping. But of course Blue stopped. He came to an easy halt as soon as I settled my weight into the saddle. And then we just stood there, reins hanging, while I petted him in long strokes on his smooth, dappled, beautiful haunches. I said, in a low voice, "Blue Blue, how are you?" and his ears flicked back and forth. I turned to the left, and, reins still loose though not dangling, asked him to canter. He lifted into an easy lope and swept down the long side of the arena. By the time I got Blue back to the barn and was taking his tack off, I had sort of forgotten about everything else. For one thing, he made me feel so much like I was out with a friend when I was on him—and when I was off him, too, since he would walk along behind me without me holding his reins. And for another, his canter put me into a dream, it was so light and smooth.

Dad came home from wherever he had been, and we rode the other horses. Lady was getting to be a pretty good reining horse. I watched Dad rope the sawcow as I was riding Oh My, and I said, "You need to get invited to work some cattle with her."

Dad nodded, then said, "Can't say I thought she had it in her, but sometimes they surprise you. Sometimes the ones who look lazy are just bored."

At supper, Dad asked me how the lessons had gone. I said, "They were good. As long as Melinda and Ellen get to see one another for a few minutes between lessons, then they both have to show me who's the best."

Mom laughed, and said, "Who's the best?"

"Well, Melinda in one way—she knows what she's doing more and is more considerate of Gallant Man. But Ellen wants to try new things and her attention never wanders. Sometimes I wish it did!"

"What about the pony?"

"Melinda is getting too big for the pony. If her stirrups are the right length, her feet hang down a little far below his chest.

I haven't said anything, though, because if her dad sells the pony, then I don't know who Ellen will ride."

Dad said, "Icelandic horses are about the same size as ponies, and adults ride them. There's a German breed, too. Blond, kind of stocky."

"I saw one of those at that show—the first one we took Gallant Man to."

Dad nodded. "I guess adults ride them, too."

"I suppose Jane will think of something."

"I suppose," said Dad.

Mom said, "You didn't ride Pie in the Sky today."

I shook my head.

There was a silence.

Dad said, "Her father did call me."

"About what?" said Mom.

"About Abby riding that horse in shows next year. Lots of shows."

I put my fork down.

Dad said, "He offered to pay her."

"How much?" said Mom.

"Thirty dollars a day."

"Oh, don't be ridiculous," said Mom.

"It's not me being ridiculous," said Dad. Now they both looked at me.

I said, "Sophia should ride her own horse."

Dad said, "Mr. Rosebury says that the two of them don't get along."

"Then they can call Jem Jarrow. He's a lot cheaper than thirty dollars a day."

"I did suggest that," said Dad.

"He doesn't really buck, not like Rally did, bound and determined to get you off. He just likes the rider to get organized and be organized."

"Well," said Dad, "If you understand that, then why don't you want to ride him?"

"Shows always go on Sunday."

"I—" But he stopped. Of course that presented a problem, but was it a thirty-dollars-a-day sort of problem?

I decided to change the subject. I said, "What would you do if a horse was prideful?"

"Prideful?" said Dad. "I don't know what you mean. A good horse does what he's told to do."

I picked up my fork and ran it around on my plate. "But do you think a horse jumps a really high course of jumps because he's told to do it?"

"Well, I guess so."

"Does Happy make those cows follow her orders because she is told to do it?"

Mom laughed.

Dad said, "Obviously, Happy has a lot of cow in her—"

"But that means she wants to do it."

Dad gave me a look, then a half smile. The look said, "You got me," but I wasn't meaning to get him, I was just meaning to understand. He said, "Yes, she wants to do it. I think it's a bossiness thing. My dad had a mare back in Oklahoma, and she was the lowest mare in the band until Uncle Luke taught her to cut cows, and then she worked her way to the top of the group by staring at the other mares and making them move, just the way she would do a cow."

"Oh, I remember her," said Mom. "She was the sweetest thing."

"Not to the other mares," said Dad.

I said, "So, she was prideful?"

"You could say she got prideful," said Dad. "She got to be a good cow horse and the boss of the mares."

Mom said, "What are you getting at, sweetie?"

I said, "Well, I wish I knew."

Dad said, "Maybe you're saying that showing a really good horse would be a way to learn something that otherwise you might not have a chance to learn, and you realize that when opportunity knocks, you should answer the door."

I shrugged. I was sure that Mr. Rosebury had talked rings around Dad, who was pretty quiet with strangers. But I also didn't know what I was saying.

Sophia was back to school on Wednesday. I saw in ancient history that she had a bag with her, of some sort of food that she was willing to eat. We had been in school for a month. Kyle gave an extra credit book report on a book called *The King Must Die*, in which the people in one of the Greek city-states killed the king every year so that the queen could marry another one, and the main character, who was named Theseus, went to Crete and was there when the earthquake destroyed the labyrinth. We then had to write a short essay on the myth we read in the myth book about Ariadne and her thread, and how this was similar or different from what Kyle talked about in his report. I wrote for a page and stopped.

What I thought was amazing was that there were so many

people in the world of the Israelites that we never talked about in church. Miss Cumberland told us that she had been to Crete and walked around the palace of Knossos one summer, and that the tiled mosaic floors were still there. However, she said that she liked the Greeks better, and that we would spend a month on them. I kept looking over at Sophia, wondering what I was going to say to her. When the bell rang, Sophia slipped out of her seat and left the room.

Our table at lunch was not one of the really big ones or good ones, but it was our table, and we all had regular places—Leslie sat at one end, with her back to the windows and her face to the door. Stella sat at the other end, because "the light was better." Mary and Luisa sat on one side, and Gloria and I sat on the other side. Sometimes I sat closer to Leslie and sometimes I sat closer to Stella. That day, I was sitting closer to Leslie, and we both saw Sophia come into the lunchroom, carrying her bag. She did not look around, she just put down her books, sat by herself, and opened her bag. Leslie said, "Where's Alana?"

She seemed to be talking to me. I said, "I don't know."

It looked like Sophia had some crackers and a carton of milk and some grapes, and she did start to eat them. Leslie said, so only I could hear her, "She needs a cupcake." Then she grinned at me. Leslie never ate cupcakes at all anymore, or candy or soda or ice cream. Stella, Gloria, and Luisa were talking about Joan Baez, and whether she was the most beautiful woman in the world. "Well," said Stella, "She's got the best hair. I saw her."

Luisa said, "People see her all the time."

Leslie moved her chair back and pulled another one over from the next table, then she waved to Sophia to come over. Sophia looked around, and, something I did not expect, she came over. She sat down on the other side of Leslie and said to me, "My dad talked to your dad. Your dad said yes."

Leslie said, "You're Sophia, right?"

Sophia reached into her bag and took out a cracker. They were Ritz crackers, round and sort of gold-colored. She said, "Right."

"I'm Leslie. You know Abby, and this is Stella, Gloria, Luisa, and Mary." And Leslie held out her hand. Sophia stared at it for a moment, then wiped her fingers on her skirt and shook it. Leslie said, "Pleased to meet you. I love your braids. We were just talking about Joan Baez. You should wear your hair down, like she does. I bet it would be longer than hers. You don't often see blond hair that long. My mom says that you are either lucky or not. Your hair grows to a certain length, and just stops growing, that's that."

Luisa said, "I'm sure mine's stopped. I measure it every month, and nothing. You're lucky, Sophia."

Sophia said, "You can call me Sophy."

She and I exchanged a glance.

Stella said, "You are very mysterious."

"Am I?"

Stella said, "Oh, yes. It's a good thing. I would love to be mysterious."

And then Leslie said, "Well, that's news to us," and we all laughed. Even Sophia smiled.

Then Stella went on, "You have some real advantages. I

mean, your clothes are basically nice quality, and you have great eyes"—Gloria kicked her under the table, but that never stopped Stella—"but a padded bra would really help."

Leslie said, "Oh, God," and Mary and Luisa rolled their eyes, but the amazing thing was that Sophia actually laughed. I had never heard her laugh, ever.

Gloria said, " Aren't you in my geometry class?"

Sophia nodded.

Gloria said, "How did you do on that test we got back?"

"I got an A minus. I missed one."

"Well, I got a C. I think you should sit with us. Stella got a D."

"Well, it wasn't an F," said Stella. "It was an improvement."

"So," said Leslie, "Stella's brain is basically nice quality, but she might have to take geometry again in the summer, which will be very bad for her swimming pool time."

"Summer is a long way away," said Stella. Then she said to Sophia, "That's a nice skirt. Two and a half inches shorter, and it would be perfect."

Sophia ate all her crackers and all her grapes. The bell rang, and she went out with Gloria and Stella to go to geometry. The next day she sat with us again, and this time Leslie did offer her something—not a cupcake, but a chocolate chip cookie. She didn't eat any of it herself, and Stella and I each ate a little piece. After lunch, I caught up with Leslie before she disappeared into the girls' bathroom, and I said, "You are being really nice to Sophia."

"Maybe."

"Well, you are."

"I mean, 'nice' makes it sound like I don't want to. I do want to."

"Why?"

"Why not? Stella is right. She's mysterious."

She went into the bathroom. Stella, Gloria, and I had never gossiped about the new Leslie. I mean, you would think that if a chubby girl whom everyone thought they knew perfectly well, and who always looks half sad sitting off to the side, goes away for the summer and comes back tall, smart, and good-looking enough that the junior boys watch her walk down the hall, that you would discuss it somehow, but maybe it was like Cinderella or Sleeping Beauty—some sort of magic happened, but you don't know what it is, so why not just accept it? I had known her since kindergarten, and I didn't even know she had a sense of humor. So it wasn't just Sophia who was mysterious.

It was that night that I found out what Mom had been worried about. I found out in the usual way, by eavesdropping, and I was pretty sorry. It was about Danny. I had been out feeding the horses, and I was on the back porch with Rusty, taking off my boots. The weather was still warm, so one of the windows was open, and I heard Mom say, "It's making me crazy." Whenever you hear your mom say something like that, then you get really quiet and don't move, partly so that she won't know you're out there, and partly so that you can hear whatever she has to say.

Mom then said, "Shouldn't he know? He never even seems

to think about it. He just takes things as they come and doesn't question them."

"What is he going to do about it?" said Dad. "Is he going to go down there and tell them to stop? They're doing him a favor."

"But someone has to take his place. Someone has to go."

I leaned forward and turned my head so my ear was close to the window screen.

"I think you're being overscrupulous. I think it's just a gift from the Lord, and we should accept it."

"How is it a gift from the Lord?"

"Well, all gifts are gifts from the Lord, but in this case, Mrs. Larkin is our sister in faith, and her cousin feels this love, and has the chance to act on it. You should be grateful. I am."

"I am grateful, but I also, oh, I don't know. I feel like this is something he, and we, will pay for in the end. It's unfair. Justice will be served. I feel like this is a sin and we are colluding in it."

Now Dad was silent, because Mom had said the most important word.

I said, "What are you talking about?"

Dad said, "Abby, are you eavesdropping?"

Mom said, "She should know. Honey, come inside, please."

I set my boots next to one another and opened the door. Mom and Dad were sitting at the table, a big bowl of shelled peas between them. Dad had the Bible in his hand, but it was closed. I sat in my chair.

Dad said, "What did you hear?"

Mom said, "You know that when Danny turned eighteen last May, he had to register for the draft, don't you?"

I nodded.

"Do you talk much at school about the war?"

I shook my head.

"Well, I guess we don't think much about it because we don't have a television and we focus more on the things of the Lord rather than the things of the world."

Dad said, "War is inevitable when the world is fallen. If you stop one, another will start. Redemption is the only path away from war."

Mom said, "But a few weeks ago, Mrs. Larkin told me something. It is that her cousin serves on the draft board, and a couple of times when Danny's name has come up, she has 'put him at the bottom of the pile.' I don't know what that means, exactly, but—"

I said, "But it's not fair to the others."

Mom nodded.

Dad said, "We don't know what motivates the cousin to do this. We don't know what the Lord has planned. Your mom hasn't talked to the cousin, and only one time to Mrs. Larkin."

"I have not been brave," said Mom.

I said, "What would happen to him?"

Mom said, "Well, he would be called up, and go to basic training, and then, depending on a lot of things, he could end up fighting in Vietnam. The thing is, since he didn't finish high school, I just think they would make cannon fodder out of him."

Dad said, "Maybe he should fight for his country."

"Maybe he should, but you and I both know that one reason we never talk about the war in church is that it's a very sore subject, and if you listen to Brother Abner, or the Hollingsworths, or any three people, for that matter, you will find out that the Lord has very strong opinions about the war, and that he does not agree with himself."

I almost laughed.

Mom said, "If he had stayed in school and then gone to college, he wouldn't even have to worry about it. He'd have a student deferment and—"

I said, "But he would be doing something that he hates."

"That he hated," said Mom. "I think maybe Leah Marx changed his mind a little. But because he was so stubborn, he doesn't get a chance to know, does he?"

I said, "He's not going to learn anything about horses in the army."

"Those days are gone," said Dad.

We all sighed at the same time.

Dad opened the Bible, and the first words his eyes fell upon were "'Give instruction to a wise man, and he will be still wiser.'"

Mom said, "I guess that means I should tell him."

Dad said, "Is Danny a wise man?"

I said, "I think so."

Mom leaned toward me, put her arm around my shoulders, and gave me a kiss. But there were tears in her eyes.

Two days later, Danny came by himself to shoe Oh My and Lady. I had already finished riding, so I held the horses while he did the job. It wasn't twilight yet, but the mountains to the west were shading the sun, so that the sky above them was almost white it was so bright. Maybe because it was near the equinox, the light was rich and the shadows of the trees so intertwined that they looked like lace. The arena was pale, and the shadow of the railing curved along it, a dark graceful line. Danny didn't say much while he was working, but then, he was leaning over the horses, hammering and shaping. Both of the mares behaved themselves very nicely, so I was proud of them. I put Lady out, and Danny put his tools away; then, while he was sweeping up hoof parings and bits of nails, I asked him about the Carmichaels. I have to admit that I was terribly curious about the Carmichaels. They were like other horse people I knew—they wore jeans and boots and had a certain way of talking that I had been around all my life, but there was also something about them that was free and easy. I said, "Where do they live?"

"Here for now."

"They're just staying here? For how long?"

"There's a cottage that's empty up by the house, so I guess Daphne sleeps in the bedroom and Ralph and Andy sleep in the living room."

"What about school?" Now I sounded like Mom.

"Daphne's in the junior high down the road. I think she's in sixth or seventh grade."

"What about Andy?"

"He's older than he looks. He just works with Ralph. They go around to other farms and train horses or work cattle. I guess they have a place, but it's too far away from anywhere."

"Where's their mom?"

"She's in Reno or somewhere like that. But she's remarried. She's got a couple of little kids. They don't see her much."

"They don't see their own mom?"

Danny turned and looked right at me, then said, "No, they don't. They've lived with Ralph since Daphne was six and Andy was thirteen."

"Are they divorced?" This was a big word.

"What do you think? Of course they are. But I guess they all get along. That's what they say. The stepdad was their vet."

I said, "Don't tell Daddy."

Danny said, "Well, he's got to learn sometime that there are all kinds of families, and all kinds of them are actually happy families. Andy says they all spend Christmas with their mom and the stepdad and the little ones every year."

I just shook my head.

In the house, I saw that we were having steak. Real steak—strip steaks that Mr. Jordan had given us after the last roundup, and mom had kept in the freezer for a special occasion. We were also having mashed potatoes and spinach, and was that a pie on top of the refrigerator? We didn't talk about much over dinner—actually the food was too good. It was like Dad said it was when he was a kid—Grandma chatted while she was cooking, everyone said how their day was while they were setting the table, but once they sat down, all they did was eat.

Finally, as she cut the apple pie she had made, Mom said, "Danny, sweetheart, I think we need to talk about something." She set his piece in front of him and he picked up his fork. Dad looked out the window. I looked out the window. Rusty was looking in the window. As she sat down, Mom said, "What's the last thing you heard from your draft board?"

Danny shrugged. "Nothing. I mean, I registered and all of that, but I don't know. I don't think much about it."

Mom said, "It's been almost five months."

"Well, it's not like there aren't a lot of guys around here. I figure that they just haven't gotten to me."

Mom said, "What are you going to do when they do get to you?"

"Go, I guess." He shrugged again.

And here was the surprising thing. Mom said, "You never thought about resisting?"

Dad's head swiveled around, and I felt mine do the same thing. But Danny wasn't surprised. He said, "I've thought of it. But—"

"But what?" said Dad.

"But first of all, I don't know if I would pass the physical or not. Andy Carmichael got called up. I guess when he was twelve, a horse fell on top of him and broke his pelvis and his shoulder, and they thought he couldn't carry equipment or march or something, anyway, he's 1-Y, and I guess if they run out of guys, they will take him."

"You've never had any accidents like that," said Dad.

"Anyway," said Danny, "I don't mind."

"You don't mind?" said Mom.

"I've thought maybe I'd like to see for myself."

Mom and Dad looked at each other, and Danny went on eating his pie. I knew there was going to be a lot of praying, and maybe even some by me, but I thought about that Bible verse Dad had found when we were talking about this, and I wondered if maybe Danny hadn't been kind of wise after all, not to say yes or no, but to want to find out about the things he didn't understand.

Mom said, "I wish you had stayed in school."

Danny said, "Even if I had, I still would not have gone to college."

We all knew this was true.

After Danny left, we sat around the living room thinking all kinds of what-if sorts of thoughts. It got so bad that about nine o'clock, I said I would go out and check the horses, even though this was normally Dad's job. I knew that when I went out, Mom and Dad would talk about things that they had not wanted to talk about in front of me. But really, Danny was eighteen; it was his business. Outside, it was cold. Maybe the first night we'd had where you had to walk fast so as not to shiver, but the light was beautiful along the hills, which were pale. Both pastures had trees in them, and the mares, at least, were lost in that darkness. I could only see a bit of Oh My's white parts flashing as she moved from place to place. Blue was standing by his gate, rummaging in the dirt for last bits of hay, so when he saw me, he knew that I was maybe going to give him a little more. He whinnied and nickered, and I petted him awhile. I even got up onto the fence and when he pushed toward me a little bit, I scratched him at the base of the neck. Morning Glory could almost scratch herself there, like a dog— she could use her back foot and scratch herself behind the ears, which I had never seen another horse do—but the base of the neck, a horse has to get someone else to do that for him.

I didn't tell him anything about Barry Boy and the Carmichaels—why get his hopes up (or mine)?—but I thought about them, and I replayed Barry Boy's lesson in my mind for the umpteenth time. I still thought it had been more fun than I had ever seen a horse have in my life, except for Happy chasing cows. I thought Blue should have some of that fun.

When I came into the house, Dad said, "Oh, by the way, I've agreed with Mr. Rosebury that you will work Pie in the Sky and take him in a show in the spring. I think it's good experience for you, and one show, for now, is not a big deal. You can ride the horse again tomorrow after you teach the girls. I have to go into town, so I'll drive you over there and pick you up. I'd like to see the horse myself. Mr. Rosebury and I can have a little chat."

He had that tone in his voice that sounds like you have no choice because this is really good for you. It made me think of a story in the Bible about a king who sees some writing on a wall, and then he knows that something is true. I saw the writing on the wall. I was going to be taking over Sophia's horse whether I wanted to or not.

Halter

Braided Rope Reins

Chapter 11

On Saturday, Sophia was wearing nice pants that were stuck into some rubber boots, and she had on a scarf, a sweater, and a jacket, even though it wasn't terribly cold. She also had a brown paper bag in her hand, and I knew there was something to eat in it, since at school, she nibbled away at grapes and apple slices and various kinds of crackers. She hadn't fainted again. She'd explained pi to Stella in a way that Stella could understand, and hypotenuse and equilateral triangle, and Stella thought she was brilliant. In the meantime, Stella explained the concept of eye shadow to Sophia. Sophia seemed less convinced than Stella, especially when Stella told her that you had to apply it at least four times a day to "maintain the freshness of the look."

At the stables, Daddy walked right up to Mr. Rosebury and they shook hands like they were trying to knock each other down. Mr. Rosebury said, "Well, Mark Lovitt, you are a legend around here. I was out of town when we picked up Onyx, but I had been planning to come out to the wilderness there and see you. Sorry I didn't! That's a great horse you sold us, and worth every penny!"

Daddy of course agreed with this, and was grinning from ear to ear. Rodney gave me a leg up onto Pie in the Sky, and after the two fathers stared at Onyx for a while, they came over and looked at us. I listened to them as I walked behind Colonel Hawkins to the arena.

"Nicely made," said Dad. "A little narrow, but a good hind-quarters on him, nice hock, good ankle."

"I like the tail set," said Mr. Rosebury. "And you know what they say about jumpers—nothing like a steep angle from the croup to the tail. Call that a 'jumping bump.'"

"Makes sense for the jumping effort," said Dad. "Horse wants to be able to open up."

"Nice long neck, too," said Mr. Rosebury. "Get a better bascule that way."

"Never heard that word before," said Dad.

"Oh, that's the arc over the jump. But to my way of thinking, different horses have different styles, and they make too much of this bascule. I like a horse like Onyx, here, who's a little flat over the top, but has plenty of spring."

Mr. Rosebury put his hand on Pie in the Sky's hip as we walked along. Once again, Jane and Sophia were behind us, lagging a little, so I couldn't hear what they were talking about.

I watched Onyx's shining black rump. His tail was waving from side to side as he walked, and when we went into the arena, he lifted it and, as Daddy would have said, "made a deposit." Truly, he was very relaxed.

Pie in the Sky was himself. I knew more or less what to do with him now, which was to put him to work moving this way and that, softening him up and getting him to pay attention. I wondered if he would put me to the test again. I was only to ride him once a week—Rodney and Colonel Hawkins were riding him three other times, but this was the only jumping day. Colonel Hawkins and Onyx trotted away from us, and I made a big loop and went the other direction. In the corner I did some small figure eights. Pie in the Sky was flat, and then he was round. His trot picked up a little spring, and he tried to canter. I think he was thinking, "Yes, I do feel pretty good this morning."

Sophia and Jane went to the center of the arena and watched us. Sophia had yet to smile, but she stared at Onyx and then at us. She looked pinched and cold.

And sad. As I trotted past her, I saw her take another cracker out of her bag.

Daddy and Mr. Rosebury kept talking the whole time that the colonel and I rode around them. They laughed, and Mr. Rosebury slapped Dad on the back three different times. I couldn't help staring a little bit. Dad had friends, but they were all in our church, and even then he was just a little stiff with them, in case someone broke a rule that he thought was important. People outside of the church were for doing business, and some he liked to do business with, such as Mr. Jordan, who was always nice; Mr. Tacker, who had bought a couple of horses from us; and Jake Morrison. But that was business. If they were not in our church, then they were not saved, and he didn't want to get too close to them or he would have to save them, and that didn't usually work (as with Uncle Luke and some of our other relatives). Mr. Rosebury didn't give him a chance, though. Every time I rode past, Mr. Rosebury was saying what a good rider I was, or what a nice horse Onyx was, or how, in another life, he wouldn't mind being the sort of horseman Dad was. Dad didn't even correct him—we have one life, and one life is one chance to do right by the Lord.

The arena we went to was the one with the outside course—you jumped over the hogback at one end, and then out into a big field. The jump at the end had been a coop, but they'd changed it, and they'd changed some of the jumps in the field, too, since the last time Onyx, as Black George, and I had tried those fences and found ourselves (a surprise to me, but not to Black George) jumping the fifteen-foot ditch. Since then, they had added two rather large brush fences and a jump that looked like a table half tilted upward. It was solid and scary-looking, but scarier to a person than a horse, since the tilt just sort of drew the horse over it. Another scary one had a ditch in front of a vertical built like a pasture fence, and another had two banks—you cantered up a slope, jumped off the bank, jumped right up onto the next bank, which was a stride away, and then galloped down that slope. Fortunately, Colonel Hawkins and Onyx took all the jumps before I did, and I could watch them. The other thing was that they were solid but not terribly high, and for Pie in the Sky that was fine. He wouldn't have touched the top of any fence if he could help it. It was fun galloping around in the grass—cross-country, you might say. He liked being out of the arena and even had a little more energy than he usually did, but because the jumps were new to him, he paid attention to them and not to whether I was offending him by not doing everything just the way he wanted me to. I didn't feel that we were about to have any refusals, and the two times he bucked a little bit seemed like exuberance rather than resistance. The jump that looked the scariest—off the one bank and onto the other—was pretty natural. Pie in the Sky was not going to get stuck between those two banks.

On the way back to the barn, Mr. Rosebury kept talking to Daddy. "Now, it's fall and the show season is over, and we can do some things for fun that we wouldn't have time to do in the spring, like play around on the outside course. These jumps are for three-day eventing. That's the colonel's first love, and it's an Olympic sport, but between you and me, there isn't a dime to be made in that sport. It's a sport for the horseman, really; old cavalry types love it. They can show off what they know to a knowledgeable audience, but I've set my sights on bigger game, if you know what I mean."

Daddy kept nodding. Either Mr. Rosebury was overwhelming him, or Daddy was making a plan, but either way, you would have thought they were best friends now.

This is not to say that Mr. Rosebury didn't pay attention to Sophia. He patted her on the head, and two or three times he peeked into her bag and made a little sign to her to keep eating. She and Jane hardly said a word to each other. When we were finished riding and were walking to the parking lot, Daddy and Mr. Rosebury were ahead of us, talking, and I walked next to Sophia. I said, "I thought the cross-country course was kind of fun, and not as scary to ride as to look at."

"I'm never scared."

"Why not?"

"I don't know. Just never was."

Now was the time to ask why she wasn't riding. We walked toward the cars, but then Dad and Mr. Rosebury stopped, and Mr. Rosebury started tapping Dad on the chest with his forefinger, while Dad nodded. I didn't want to hear what they were saying, so I stopped, too. This was when I said, "So why not ride?"

Sophia just shrugged. But then she said, "The more they want me to, the less I want to." She cocked her head at her father, and I realized he had the same effect on me. It was like every word was a little prod of some sort, nudging you toward whatever he thought you should do. At least Dad and Mom were straightforward: "You will do this, and I'm not going to discuss it." You could do it or not, but if you didn't do it, you knew what the consequences would be, and if you did do it, well, whatever it was was over and done with. But for Mr. Rosebury, nothing was ever over, because he always had bigger plans. I thought maybe I should give up on Sophia.

Dad was in a good mood as we drove home. He hummed a couple of tunes that he liked, "Red River Valley" and "Banks of the Ohio." We knew these songs, and I always thought it was funny that he sang them when he was happy, because they were sad songs. He didn't say much to me about Pie in the Sky, other than "That horse ever turned out?"

"I don't think so."

"He might like that. He seems full of beans."

"I guess they think he's too valuable for that. I mean, he gets ridden four days a week, and maybe Rodney lunges him the other three."

"Never could see that way of thinking, myself." He shook his head. "Horse has to have time to be a horse."

I went out and tacked up Blue and took him through the mare pasture down to the crick. Oh My and Nobby walked along with us and Rusty went ahead—at one point, I could hear her bark three times, and then I heard some rustling. If there was rustling, then she was chasing a deer, which she did just for exercise. Blue ambled along, happy to be out, and for sure happy to have some company going along with us. It was always true that when Oh My was relaxed, then the other horses were relaxed also because she was the boss mare of the little band. When we got down to the crick, Oh My splashed around in the six inches of water that was still running; Nobby even got down and rolled, since the bottom of the crick right there was sandy and cool. Blue seemed to enjoy their company. He dipped his nose in the water and splashed once or twice before taking a small drink, then he pawed a couple of times. I could tell that he felt very comfortable. I sat deep in the saddle and stroked him over the top of his haunches. Oh My was like Leslie, wasn't she? She told everyone what to do, but in a relaxed way. Blue had friends. Probably Pie in the Sky did not have friends—Sophia wasn't his friend, and I wasn't his friend, and the way he lived at the stables meant that he didn't have a chance to make horse friends.

* * *

Sophia now sat with us at lunch every day, and Alana sat across the room, by the window, with Linda A., whom we had gone to school with, and some new friends of hers that she had met working on the school newspaper and the yearbook. Leslie had made a rule that if Sophia saw something in our lunches that looked good to her, she could eat it, and that person would get a bonus point for letting her have it.

So every day we would take our lunches out of the sacks and Sophia would look at them, and sometimes she picked something. When she did, we all laughed. But Leslie gave her a rule, too—she had to eat it. It was actually kind of fun, and I found that when I was deciding what to put in my lunch in the morning, I looked for things that Sophia might possibly choose. The one I came up with was dried apricots. Stella came up with Fig Newtons. Leslie herself came up with carrot sticks dipped in cream cheese. Lucia brought popcorn from the night before. Sophia's eyes actually got big when she saw that, and she ate it right up. We had no idea what we would do with the bonus points, but we figured that Leslie would come up with something.

It was Leslie who told me that there was a bus that went from the high school past the Marble Ranch, stopping on the way to pick up kids at the junior high. If I wanted to go to the Marble Ranch, that was the one I would take. I decided not to wait any longer and, on Tuesday, called Mom from the office. She said it was okay.

When the kids got on at the junior high school, Daphne got on almost last and sat down in the front. But the bus driver took off pretty fast and we all had to stay seated, so I couldn't let her know I was there. It was interesting to watch her, though. She sat next to the window, smiling and looking out at the passing scenery. She talked a little bit to the girl next to her, but it didn't seem like they were good friends. Then, after we had been going for about five minutes, a paper wad hit the window above her head, and she turned around. Just as the bus driver looked in the mirror and shouted, "Hey, back there! George Kennedy, I see you!" another paper wad flew in Daphne's direction, and her hand went up and caught it, just like that. She gave it to the girl next to her, who leaned forward and gave it to the bus driver, who called out, "I'm taking this to the police, and they are going to fingerprint this!"

I don't think anyone believed him, but the kids did quiet down. Daphne went back to looking out the window.

When we got to the stop, she got off without realizing that I was behind her, but when I stepped down from the bus, she exclaimed, "Oh, Abby! Hi! Were you really on the bus?"

"I was in the back."

We started up the road.

I said, "That was neat, the way you caught that paper wad."

She grinned. "That bus is crazy. Some of those boys were talking about putting a bag over the bus driver's head one day."

"They never did it, did they?"

"I would have tripped them if I saw them coming."

"I bet you would have."

The arena was empty, so we walked all the way up the hill to the barn, and I followed Daphne into the office, then into a small courtyard. It was a windy spot, and the oaks were huge—they loomed over the barns and the leaves rattled, but the view was wide and imposing, with the Marble Ranch valley just beneath us, then a deeper valley, and steep, dark green mountains beyond that. Daphne took her books into one of the cabins, and as I was looking around, Danny emerged from one of the others (there were three), and of course he was surprised to see me. It was almost four thirty by the stable clock. I said, "Is that your room?"

He nodded.

"Can I see it?"

But he ignored me, which I expected him to do. Even when he was living at home and he was twelve and I was eight, he had a sign on his door that said, "Do Not Entire!" When he didn't answer, I poked him in the ribs, and he laughed, but he still didn't take me to see it. I said, "I want to watch the Carmichaels some more."

"I guess Daphne is going to ride, and I suppose you can watch. But how are you going to get home?"

I knew Danny would take me. But I didn't say anything. Daphne came out in her riding clothes, with two apples in her hands. She said, "You want one of these? They're Sierra Beauties. Pop knows a guy who sends them to us."

I took the apple, and tasted it. It was really good. Danny said, "Hey! Aren't you going to even give me a bite?"

I gave him a bite. Then she said, "I guess they're down there? The bus was a little slow today."

Danny said, "Well, someone brought a horse from up in Watsonville. I shod him, too. But only in front."

"Oh," said Daphne. "That's Curly. He's fun. Pop coaches him once a month. Mr. Pinckney brings him to us, wherever we are."

I said, "How much does your dad charge?"

"Well," said Daphne, "he charges a half peck of onions, some pork chops, a couple of pork roasts, some garlic, and some lettuce. Mr. Pinckney has a farm up there. He brings stuff."

I said, "Would he take money?"

Danny and Daphne both laughed.

As we came down, we could see someone letting Curly into the arena. He trotted around a little bit, then whinnied. Curly was little and almost black, only about the size of Morning Glory, but muscular and strong-looking. Ralph was standing with the owner, talking. Daphne called out, "Hey, Pop!"

He gave her a big smile, and the owner shouted, "Hey, Daphne, how are ya, darlin'?"

Daphne began to run, and Danny and I sped up.

We followed the three of them and the horse to the training paddock. I guess Daphne had been riding and training Curly for a while—he was a mature horse and fit. He walked along on a loose rein with his tail swinging back and forth, but he had his eye out. He looked alert and self-confident. When they got to the pen, I saw that the jumps were pretty high, and there were a lot of poles stacked in the center of the paddock. Daphne spent about ten minutes warming the little horse up, mostly on a loose rein, but she did ask him, bit by bit, to lift his head and lengthen his stride. When they were finally going, he looked like a picture in a book, stepping lively, his neck arched and his ears pricked. Just about then, Andy showed up.

When Daphne started the jumping part, she picked up a real gallop, not a canter. The difference was not in the horse's level of excitement, or even the quickness of his strides, but in his stride length. He went at a good pace around the arena, changing directions, changing leads, slowing down, speeding up. He handled his body as well as I had ever seen a horse do, and Daphne stuck right with him. She galloped down over the fences that Ralph and the owner had built for her, and she did it on her own—Ralph didn't call out and tell her what to jump. The effect of this was to make the whole thing seem more fun. She was doing what she felt like (and the horse felt like) without being ordered about.

She must have taken fourteen or sixteen jumps, first at about 3'3" and then about 3'6". Ralph and Andy just went around, staying out of her way, and raised the jumps. Then she came to the trot and let the horse stretch his head and neck down and move out. The horse trotting was like a baseball player or some other kind of athlete stretching himself a little after making an effort. Then they walked. While they were taking a break, Ralph and Andy and the owner started moving the poles. Danny and I went in to help them when we saw what they were doing.

They were building a long chute that ran around half of the pen, and inside the chute, at intervals, were jumps, just poles, but high—3'9" and 4'. It took us about ten minutes to complete the whole thing, and Daphne spent some of that time trotting and turning; she was always moving. When we were finished with the chute, we backed away, and Ralph went over to Curly, who was standing near the front of the chute, and removed his bridle. Curly picked up his trot and then his gallop and galloped down through the chute, jumping the jumps, and Daphne spread her arms out like wings, the way I often had Barbie Goldman and the girls do at the walk. And she jumped the jumps in perfect rhythm. Curly did not have to be asked twice—he kept going around the pen after he was out of the chute, and went right down through it and over the jumps again. I was impressed, and so was Danny—he was staring with his mouth a little open and his eyebrows raised. I whispered, "Did you ever see this before?" and he shook his head. I guess Curly was the first trained jumper he had seen the Carmichaels work with; other than him, it was all green horses.

They raised the jumps yet again, and Daphne and the horse did it once more. This time, Daphne had one hand on her chest and one over her head. She was like a circus rider.

It was pretty clear that Curly had his own style. He did not arc over the fence quite as nicely as Barry Boy—he popped over it and kicked his back legs. If he took the wrong lead, Daphne did not force him to change back, but waited until he realized that things were easier if he was on the proper lead. In fact, it looked like Curly was so sure of what he was doing that Daphne was more or less along for the ride. Andy came over to us, and I said, "How high can that horse jump?"

"Well, he's done a five-foot course, but only a couple of times."

"Who rode him?"

"I did."

Danny said, "Where did Mr. Pinckney get him?"

"You want to know?"

We nodded.

"Got him from a pony ride place. These little kids would get on him, and then they would get buckled in, and the horses would trot around a kind of grid. Mr. Pinckney didn't really know why he bought him—he's got a ranch but no horses, only trees and vegetables and fruits. But he had a feeling, and so he brought him home. One day, when Curly was feeling frisky, he jumped out of his pen and trotted down the road to make friends, and the place he went, those people knew us, so they suggested Mr. Pinckney give dad a call."

"Should have named him Jack in the Box," said Danny.

"He does show a couple of times every year, but he's mostly a pet. Mr. Pinckney built him a stall off the back of their house, and he's allowed to put his head in the window and have treats."

I said, "I wish we could do that. Dad doesn't even allow the dog in the house."

Andy walked away, and Daphne took Curly out for a walk around the big arena. We started taking down the chute, and I said to Danny, "I want Blue to do this."

"That would be fun."

"No, I mean it. I want to bring Blue over and have some lessons. I'll pay. That guy Peter Finneran charged sixty dollars. I'll pay that."

"Do you have that?"

"In—"

"Will Dad let you spend that?"

I shrugged. It was one of those let-him-try-and-stop-me shrugs.

Then Danny said, "Well, but they might be leaving. I think I heard them say—"

I walked right over to Ralph Carmichael, and I said, "Mr. Carmichael, I want some lessons with you more than anything in the world. I will pay you sixty dollars, and do it anytime you like. I have a wonderful sweet horse—he's a Thoroughbred and he has a great canter, and this is exactly what he needs."

Ralph looked a little startled, and actually stroked and curled the right side of his mustache. Then he said, "Well, when do you have in mind?"

"Danny says you might be leaving?"

"We've got some plans to get down to Los Angeles in a bit." He looked at me for a long moment, but it wasn't the way most grown-ups look at you, as if you had better do something or else. He had brown eyes under the white eyebrows. After a moment, he said, "Oh, sorry. I was just thinking." He shook his head. Then he said what grown-ups always say: "We'll see."

I said, "I have sixty dollars. Danny can bring Blue over here and take him home. You can decide how many lessons sixty dollars is worth."

Mr. Carmichael smiled and said again, "We'll see."

Danny did take me home. He grumbled about it, but it turned out he wanted to talk to Daddy about taking Happy to a roundup, and then there was fried chicken for supper, and so why not?

The thing with grown-ups is that you have to get them to think that something you want is their idea. And anyway, I was still excited about what we had seen, so as soon as everyone was sitting at the table, I said, "A guy brought his horse down from Watsonville for Ralph Carmichael to train, and he was about the size of Morning Glory and he jumped four feet." I glanced at Danny, then said, "He's just a pet, but Andy says he's jumped him over five-foot courses a couple of times."

I allowed this to sink in, and then Danny said, "Ralph's idea is that horses are a lot better jumpers than we think they are. We just don't train them to enjoy it."

Mom said, "Five feet! I don't think—"

I said, "Daphne did the highest jumps without even a bridle."

Mom said, "Did it break?"

"No." Danny lifted his eyebrows. "Ralph removed it. I've seen them do that once before."

Dad said, "Horses can do lots of things without bridles. My mare used to cut cattle without a bridle." I had forgotten this.

Danny said, "Ralph likes them to be as free as they can be. When he—" He glanced at me. "Well, you'll see."

"See what?" said Mom.

"You'll see how he does it when Abby takes Blue over there and has a lesson or two."

"Blue is certainly not ready for—"

I said, "No, but most of the horses they train over there are beginners. Three- and four-year-olds off the track. They do little things. But they like it."

"That clinic you already went to was expensive," said Dad, "and I'm not sure it was good value for the—"

"I have money."

"Yes, but—"

"I want to invest in my horse. If he's going to be sold eventually, then he has to be as good as possible."

Dad stared at me.

"What we're doing isn't working," I went on. After a pause, I added, "It's my money."

Danny waited for a long silent moment, then said, "You should come and watch. It's about as much fun as you've ever seen a horse having."

And Dad said, "Okay."

That was the first step.

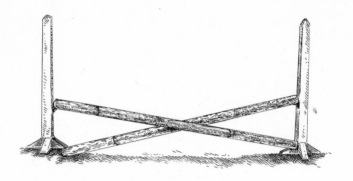

Crossbar Jump

Coiled Lasso

Chapter 12

After Danny left, I did what I had to do—that meant that I went up to my room and turned on Simon and Garfunkel. That also meant that I left Mom and Dad to talk about my lessons with Ralph Carmichael on their own, no nagging from me. So, I employed some magic charms: I worked out all twenty geometry problems and both of the extra-credit ones. I wrote my one-page paper on the myth of Sisyphus, which was about a guy who pushes a rock up a hill every day, only to have it roll back down every night. I read the first two chapters of *David Copperfield*, which I had not been looking forward to ever since we read another book by Charles Dickens, *Great Expectations*. *David Copperfield* looked like more of the same, only longer, and we would be reading it for four weeks. I also studied for my test on the differences between magma, pumice, basalt, lava, and tephra. I memorized where the volcanoes were: the Pinnacles, thirty miles away, which hadn't erupted in twenty-five million years, and Mount Shasta, which erupted in 1786. The teacher said that we would get to earthquakes next week, which I was not looking forward to. In French, we had finished the book about the red balloon and were now memorizing irregular verbs: *je dors, tu dors, il dort, nous dormons, vous dormez, ils dorment. Je couvre, tu couvres, il couvre*, and so forth. I yawned. *Hello darkness my old friend, I've come to talk with you again.* This line made no sense to me, but what with the *dormir* and the *couvrir* and a long day, I went to sleep with the lights on and the music playing.

Daddy was up and sitting at the table when I came in from giving the horses their morning hay. He was so excited that he and his chair were practically hopping around the floor as he poured sugar into his coffee cup, and as soon as I sat down he said, "Guess what?"

"What?"

"Ralph Carmichael has agreed to give you a lesson—really two lessons, or maybe three, but two anyway—"

I threw my arms around his neck. I could not believe that all the charms had worked so quickly and so well.

"And you don't have to pay, because we'll do the lessons on Pie in the Sky and Mr. Ro—"

I sat down again and closed my mouth, which had dropped open. "What?"

"I told him last night about what you said about that little horse jumping five feet, and I could hardly—"

"I wasn't talking about Pie in the Sky."

"Jane will certainly want to come watch, and may bring some other horses and riders, depending on how it goes. I can't help thinking that the Lord is at work here, giving us this opportunity. Ralph is happy to do—"

Well, I didn't scream. But I did growl.

Daddy looked startled for a moment, then said, "I know your first idea was to take Blue."

I said, "That was my only idea."

"Blue doesn't have the poten—"

"I don't care."

"Of course you care. It's essential to invest where it will make the most—"

I got up and walked out of the kitchen and up to my room, where I changed my clothes. This time I was ten minutes early for the school bus.

Sophia didn't say a thing about this in ancient history, even though she sat next to me and told me how the night before, at supper, her dad's Gordon setter went into the kitchen while they were eating in the dining room, put his paws on the counter, and stole what was left of the chicken, but then he tried to get it through the dining room to his bed in her dad's study by turning his head as he passed the table so they wouldn't see that he had it. When she told me this, we laughed out loud in spite of the death of Socrates, and Miss Cumberland gave us a very dirty look. I decided to remember this to tell to Barbie in the letter I intended to write. But Sophia didn't seem to know then, or at lunch, about the Carmichaels.

It is very annoying the way that grown-ups are always so sure that they know best, and whatever you say you really

215

want to do or have to do, they take as a suggestion. And then, if you are not grateful at how your plan sort of got lost in theirs, they get mad. All day long at school, I knew perfectly well that Dad, Mr. Rosebury, Jane, Colonel Hawkins, and Mr. Carmichael were concocting some clinic that would suit them but that would not be at all like Barry Boy and Blue and Curly cantering and playing in the paddock at the Marble Ranch toward twilight, with the hills cool and peaceful all around us, and the grass and the trees dark and mysterious. Not at all like that.

When I got home, I went straight upstairs, put on my riding clothes, and headed to the barn. I heard Mom call my name from the kitchen, but I pretended that I didn't. Blue was standing over the water trough with Lincoln, and they were staring at something. When I looked, I saw a dead squirrel lying on the bottom. Sometimes the squirrels perch on the edge to try to get a drink but fall in and drown. If they do, even though it's gross, you have to dump out the water trough and scrub it, and of course you have to do something with the squirrel. This one wasn't too swollen, so it hadn't been in there very long. I picked it up with the shovel and carried it over to the manure pile and pushed it way under, then covered it with manure and straw. It's disgusting, but it's the healthiest way to get rid of them and the best way to make sure that Rusty wouldn't decide that the squirrel was her business. Even so, that meant another hour before I could get Blue out of the pasture and start with him, and it made me impatient somehow— I kept looking at Nobby and thinking I had to ride her, too, and maybe Morning Glory. My time was being wasted. It was getting late, and then I couldn't find Blue's bridle, and had to look for that.

How mad I was felt like waves, hot boiling waves, just rolling out of me over everything, even the things I wasn't mad at, like the sunshine spreading through the mare pasture, and the mares themselves, and Mom, of course, and Rusty, who was now sitting quietly on the back porch while Mom lifted each of her feet, wiped them off, and then clipped her toenails. I could have named you twenty-five things I was mad about, like Peter Finneran sneering at Blue and saying, "One down, four to go" when he'd chased Sophia out of the arena, so mean. I was mad about how the adults didn't seem to care how he talked to us, and how Peter Finneran himself probably thought he was a wonderful person. I was mad about Barbie and Alexis going away to school, and our school not being good enough for them. I was mad about Sophia never acting like a regular person. I was mad about Danny being sad about Leah going to college, and I was mad about Danny getting drafted and probably, possibly, maybe going off to war. I was mad about having to read *David Copperfield* when no one, no one, had said that they liked *Great Expectations*. And I was mad that I was mad about so many stupid things. But of course, I was mostly mad that Daddy and Mr. Rosebury were doing my idea their way, and Blue was being lost in the shuffle. And I was mad that they thought my idea wasn't really my business, now that they'd taken it over.

I sat down on the tack trunk, and because I knew I couldn't scream, I made a whole bunch of faces in a row, some of them silent screaming, some of them scowling, some of them sticking out my tongue, and some of them baring my teeth. If I had had horse ears, I would have pinned them. By the time Mom came into the barn, I was just sitting there.

She was humming a little tune, not anything I knew, maybe not even a real song, just some notes. Rusty was tagging along behind her and sniffing this and that. Rusty's interest in every detail of our place was never-ending. After Mom nested the bucket she was carrying into two others, she got the rake and started raking up bits of hay. When she was done she came over and kissed me on the forehead, then turned and walked out. I was really glad she didn't say anything.

You are never supposed to ride your horse in a temper, even if you think you have controlled your temper, so I took the halter and got Blue, but after I put him in the cross-ties, all I did was brush him in long strokes, especially with the soft brush, top to toe and front to back. I took time with his belly, making sure I got it clean, but also making sure not to bother him. Horses' bellies are sensitive. I felt exhausted. I closed my eyes.

When I opened them again the first thing I saw was Daddy's truck coming over the hill that was about half a mile from our gate. It was the one spot on the road that you could see from the barn. I was no longer tired. I got my saddle and Blue's bridle. I did not want to see Dad. I was too mad at him. I put on Blue's saddle, girthed him up, put on the bridle, and got on. I was past the paddocks before Daddy was through the gate. I got around the bend in the trail, and then I slowed down. The question was where to go. I wanted a long ride.

So I went through a little gate between our place and the Jordan Ranch. We almost never used this gate—I had to dismount and open it, because the latch and the hinges were rusted—but once in a while we did ride through that part of the ranch. Mr. Jordan had said that we could, but Daddy didn't like us to do it too often. The most neighborly thing to do was go there a few times a year, to show that we accepted his hospitality, but no more than that, so as not to take advantage.

Was I still mad? Yes, but not generally, not at Blue or Mom. I was just mad at Daddy and Mr. Rosebury. But I was really mad at them. I got back on Blue and we turned right, along one of the ranch roads. Blue flicked his ears and turned his head. I looked back. There was Rusty, sliding under the fence and trotting after us, her tail waving in the air. Rusty loved a chance to explore.

This was a nice open trail that went diagonally up a big hill. It leveled out, and then there was an undulating stretch that was good for a bit of a canter. There were a few oaks here and there, but mostly the hillside was dry, golden grass. The cattle that had been here in the spring had been moved to give the pasture a rest, so it was very quiet. Blue picked up a lively trot and then a perfect rocking canter. I had him on a light rein. He was calm but alert, his ears moving and his head turning this way and that. I understood that he really was a Thoroughbred—knowing what you are doing at the gallop (and now we were galloping) was what a Thoroughbred was born to do. I felt it in my body that his body was completely relaxed. We galloped and galloped, and we lost sight of Rusty, but if anyone could take care of herself, it was Rusty.

There were two forks in the road, and both times I galloped down the wider, flatter fork, not so much paying attention to where I was going, only to which road had the smoother surface. The air was fresh and blew in my face. My hair sort of fluttered around under my hard hat, and Blue's mane fluttered, too. I could see his forelock between his ears, wafting up and down. We were going fast, maybe, but it just felt smooth and endless. We went around a couple more hills, and over another one, too, and then Blue finally slowed down, not as if he was tired, but more as if he was no longer bubbly. When we came down to the walk, he walked along quite happily, still looking, still moving his ears. I sighed and realized that I had been smiling. I was panting a little and laughing, too. I wasn't angry anymore, not at Daddy, not even at Mr. Rosebury, who was way more annoying than Daddy. Then I realized that I didn't know where I was. And that it was getting dark.

At first, neither of these last two things bothered me, because I was so relieved at the first one. The thing is, sometimes when you are feeling really good, it takes you a while to put two and two together and come up with something as simple as four. In this case, four was that I was in trouble. How big was the Jordan Ranch? Was it five thousand acres or ten thousand acres? Whatever it was, it was so big that whenever anyone said the number, I sort of blanked out, since I couldn't imagine that many acres.

I looked around in the deepening twilight. There was lighter sky off over one set of hills. That would be west. And the entrance to the Jordan Ranch was east of our place, but the ranch itself curved around our place, and was sometimes to the north of it and sometimes, if you got far enough, to the west of it. So where I had to go depended on where I was, and I had no idea where I was. I decided that the only solution was to re-trace my steps, so I turned around and went back along the road I was on. Obviously, since I'd only taken two forks, when I came to those forks, I would keep going more or less straight, and end up back on the road that went through the gate.

Except what if there were forks in the road that I hadn't noticed because we were galloping? There were all sorts of what-ifs, in fact. What if no moon? I couldn't remember if there had been a moon lately, or when it had risen if there was one. Also, what if a bear, a mountain lion, a bobcat, a rattle-snake, or coyotes? Well, there weren't any bears that I had heard of. I focused on that and did not let myself think of the worst thing, which was the rattlesnake. I had seen a rattlesnake once, and Danny had seen a rattlesnake once. There was a story Danny told us about Jake Morrison, who had been riding up a trail along a cliff at his place, and a rattlesnake slithered off the cliff, over his horse's neck in front of the horn of the saddle, and down to the ground. Jake was so surprised he didn't even get scared until after the snake was gone. I said, "Blue, watch out for snakes."

Just then, there was a sudden *hoooooo*, and an owl flew over me. It was that dark.

But the path was light. The sky was darker than the ground, and Blue seemed to be walking along without any problem. Horses see fine in the dark, actually. He came to what I thought was the second fork we had taken and I looked around. We had gone to the right, so now we were heading a little more to the west. I looked behind us. I could just see the curve of the trail. If I had gone northwest and now I was going east and south, that made sense. We walked along. The crickets started. Then there were some coyote howls, first fairly far away, and then fairly close, off to my right, between me and our place. I shivered, whether from fear or from cold I didn't know. Blue didn't seem to care about the coyote howls—he flicked his ears but didn't even look. Probably he heard coyotes howling every night. We kept going. I sort of remembered that the first fork I had taken had been to the left. But the road gave me no clues. The coyotes howled again, and this time I saw them, two of them, maybe a hundred yards away, silhouetted against the pale field, their noses pointed upward, and then another howl pierced the darkness. Blue threw his head back, pricked his ears, and snorted. All of a sudden, I was afraid.

But then there was a bark, and here came Rusty, arrowing along in the grass, *bark bark bark,* chasing those coyotes away. Blue bounced once in surprise, but he surely recognized Rusty and her activities, because once she had chased off the coyotes, she came and walked along beside us, her head down and her tail down as if she was tired, and he relaxed, too. I guess she had had a busy time. After she joined us, I was no longer afraid, though I don't know why. Maybe I had read *Lassie Come-Home* enough times to trust her, and anyway, Rusty came home every night from all sorts of adventures. I let Blue follow her, and soon we got to the first place that the road forked, then the flat area where we had started galloping, then the hillside where we went down to the left, and then, in the distance, I saw the gate.

We were all tired by this time. I got off to open and close

the gate, and I didn't get back on. I knew it would take longer to get home, but it was a relief to walk and stretch those muscles. It also kept me warmer. Blue and Rusty walked along with me. I guess it was pretty late when we got to the barn, and I knew one thing—that I was in trouble.

But, to be honest, I was too tired to care about much of anything. I untacked Blue and put him in the stall so that he could eat some hay by himself—I would put him out with Lincoln before I went to bed. There was no clock in the barn, so I didn't know what time it was. I could have been gone for two hours or three; I had no idea. I supposed they would tell me.

On the porch, I took off my boots. Then I opened the door. The kitchen light was on, the dishes were done, my plate was on the table. The clock above the sink said a quarter to eight. That was pretty late, but it wasn't midnight. I slammed the door. I figured they would want to know I was back.

It was Dad who appeared in the doorway. He said, "Go up to your room after you eat. We'll talk about this tomorrow."

Well, it was back to doing everything right—cleaning up, homework, reading, staring out the window at Lincoln, the only horse I could see, contemplating my sins. But really, whatever they were going to say, getting lost with Blue on the Jordan Ranch didn't feel like a sin. It felt like an adventure. And I didn't see how Dad was going to convince me otherwise.

I was already in bed, listening to the Mamas and the Papas and half asleep, when Mom knocked and came in. She sat on the bed. She said, "Did you run away?"

"No. I just didn't realize how late it was. I went for a ride on the Jordan Ranch and got a little lost. Is Dad really mad?"

"He was sure something had happened to you."

"What about you?"

"I thought you were fine. I mean, Blue was gone, Rusty was gone. I knew you were all together."

"How come you don't worry all that much and Dad does?"

Mom leaned forward and whispered, "I believe a little more in grace and he believes a little more in sin." She hugged me. Then she looked me right in the face and said, "You should know, Abby, that your dad started crying when he thought you were, I don't know, gone somehow. I can't remember the last time I saw him cry. Maybe when we were kids. But he doesn't want to lose you. He really doesn't."

Like he lost Danny, I thought.

I said, "Can you put Blue back out?"

"Sure."

It's really not good to talk about these kinds of things before you go to bed, because you spend the whole night, both dreaming and waking, arguing with yourself. I mean, I even had a dream where I was writing a chart, which was yellow and looked like a crossword puzzle, where the words running down were why I was mad at Daddy and the words running across were why he was mad at me. When I woke up after this dream, I was absolutely sure that the words running down outnumbered the words running across, but I couldn't remember what any of them were, so I lay there half asleep and thought of Blue, the Carmichaels, Sophia. But of course Daddy had nothing to do with Sophia. Yes, Sophia had my old horse, Black George, but now that I had Blue and had ridden Pie in the Sky, Black George—Onyx—seemed a little uninteresting to me. Blue was much more my friend, and Pie in the Sky was more of a challenge. I mean, you ride a horse and you have to think hard in order to solve the problem of him, and when you do, it is so exciting that other horses who never present problems don't make you as happy.

But that was a lesson, too—when we sold Black George, I was really upset and thought that maybe I would never get over it, and here I was, over it. On the other hand, that's what grown-ups always wanted you to think, that you would get over whatever you were upset about. Plus there was a part of me that knew I was right about my idea of taking Blue to Ralph Carmichael, and because I was right, I didn't want to get over it. I had been doing as I was told for years and years—my whole life. All around me, there were kids not doing as they were told. Did I really want to be one of those kids?

I closed my eyes and started counting backward from a thousand in order to go to sleep without answering this question. I did go to sleep. The last number I remember thinking was thirty-two.

When I woke up in the morning, the first thing I thought about was being out in the nighttime with Blue. Things I hadn't realized that I'd noticed came into my mind—the first stars brightening to the east, only a few scattered across the sky above the blackness of the mountains; the pale grass, which in some places looked flat white and in other places looked shadowed and deep; Blue's neck, almost luminous, splattered with dark spots, his ears glinting somehow as they flicked back and forth; his breathing, which I could feel between my calves and hear, too; the sound of the crickets, which at first seemed like silence and then became a chorus of tiny noises; Rusty aiming for the coyotes, and their dark figures skittering away. When I got up to put on my clothes, yawning and thinking of these things, I was in a pretty good mood. But then I saw that my books and papers were still spread over my desk, and I know I would have to hurry up in order to get ready for school.

I stumbled down the stairs, pushing my hair out of my face, and went out the back door. Sometime soon Daylight Saving Time would end, and it would be light in the morning again. I would be happy about that.

Well, there was Daddy, in the dark barn, throwing flakes of hay into the wheelbarrow. He turned when I stepped through the door, and right then and there I said, "Daddy, I am sorry that I went off and got kind of lost last night. I was mad about something, but I really wasn't intending to keep Blue out after dark. I know that was dumb. I'm sorry."

Why did I say this when I had just been thinking how strange and enjoyable the whole experience had been? Well, he looked at me. He looked right at me, and I felt bad that he had worried about me and that he had cried. I just did. He said, "Apology accepted." And then he didn't say anything more. If he had been Mr. Rosebury, he would have gone on and on about it, but he was Daddy, and whatever was true about me and Blue getting lost in the night, it was over now.

He pushed the wheelbarrow and I threw the hay to the horses, first the mares and then the two geldings, and when we went in the house, Mom had made toast and oatmeal. As we ate, Daddy said, "Joe Tacker bought a five-year-old at a sale in

Modesto and wants to send him over here to be retrained. Purebred quarter horse out of Quo Vadis."

"You're kidding!" said Mom. "She was—"

"I'm sure he spent a pile on this one," said Dad. "I guess we'll be staring at him all the time, just to see what he's got."

"How much are you going to charge him?"

"Seventy-five dollars board, seventy-five training."

I said, "Does that mean we don't have to sell Oh My yet?"

Mom smiled. Dad nodded.

The only other thing that happened was that when I came down the stairs after changing my clothes and getting my books, he stopped me and kissed me on the top of the head as I went out the door. I gave him a hug around the waist.

The clinic, such as it was, had to be done in a hurry, because the Carmichaels were leaving for Southern California in two weeks. I spent the next four days not looking forward to it. It was going to take place out at the stables on Saturday and Sunday. Mr. Rosebury persuaded Dad to let me take Pie in the Sky both days. Even on short notice, Jane had rounded up five more participants, including someone from Santa Rosa. Andy was going to bring Barry Boy, and Daphne was going to ride Curly. So that would be eight, and how they were going to divide us up I had no idea. That was the mystery of Ralph Carmichael: he did things his own way. Sophia said nothing about it at school, and I didn't ask her. Once or twice I thought I might, but when I looked at her and opened my mouth, instead I asked her about *The Iliad* and *The Odyssey*, since on Friday we were having our test on the Greeks.

Friday night, I cleaned my boots. Mom had already washed my breeches. I had a nice sweater and a jacket in case it was cold. That was all I had to do. Rodney would do the rest, which was fine with me. Mr. Rosebury was even paying for the clinic, so my bank account would remain untouched. As for Melinda and Ellen, Jane thought it would do them a world of good to watch, and so she called their moms and invited them. Melinda said she didn't know, and Ellen said she would bring her riding clothes. I had to laugh at that.

The Carmichaels weren't like Peter Finneran, expecting us to be there on the dot and saluting at 9:00 a.m. Ten o'clock was fine, and whoever was there would get started; the others could take their time. We were given not the big arena right out front but a smaller one back near the trees. When I led Pie in the Sky around the barns and back there, at first I didn't see anyone; then I saw Ralph, a cup of coffee in his hand, leaning against the fence and looking into the woods. When we came through the gate, he pointed out a woodpecker, then sipped his coffee, then strolled around Pie in the Sky taking a look at him. He smoothed his mustache, turned, and strolled back the other way. About then, Andy brought Barry Boy in. Ralph said to me, "Why don'tcha take the tack off that horse. Give him a chance to run around a bit."

I said, "He may not have done that since he was a colt."

"'Bout time, then," said Ralph.

The first thing that Pie in the Sky did was lie down in the sand and roll. He rolled, stood up, lay down, rolled on the other side, stood up, trotted across the arena to an especially wet spot, and lay down and rolled over and back, grunting as he did it. When he stood up, Ralph said, "Back's a little suppler now." Pie in the Sky then trotted along the far fence line, staring at horses in one of the other arenas, and then he leapt in the air, kicked up, and took off snorting. I said, "What if he hurts himself?"

"Ah, he's not that type. Look at him. He's agile and he knows what he's doing. Now, you can have two horses run down a hill, and one of them judges wrong and runs into the fence, and the other one, even if the ground is slippery, he shifts his weight and slides, and he stops about a foot before the fence. Never touches it. This horse is like that."

I said, "He's a good jumper."

"That's what they say."

Now Barry Boy came trotting over. He snuffled noses with Pie in the Sky, and then Pie in the Sky arched his neck, lifted his tail, and trotted away from him, which meant that Pie in the Sky was saying, "I'm the boss," and when Barry Boy lifted his tail, Ralph lifted the flag he had next to him (which was really just a whip with a scarf attached to the tip) and moved them out—better to make them go than let them argue.

They started galloping and romping, and even when Pie in the Sky kicked out, he just stretched his leg toward Barry Boy, and Barry Boy moved aside. After that, they cantered about, then Pie in the Sky trotted away to look at the other horses who were coming toward the arena, and Barry Boy got down and rolled in the sand. Ralph said, "Well, they like this sand, and I don't blame them. Got to scratch where it itches."

Now everyone was here—Daphne and Curly, Nancy with Parisienne, and three other girls that I had seen around the barn. Everyone's horses were neatly brushed and tacked up. When Andy came along and said, "Okay, let's get the tack off these animals and let them play for ten minutes," all the girls except Daphne looked at each other, but one by one they turned their horses loose. Ralph went into the center of the arena with his flag, and Andy went over by the gate. Daphne and I took the other girls out of the arena and over to where Jane, Dad, Mr. Rosebury, Rodney, and a couple of other people I didn't know were leaning on the fence. One of the girls said, "I don't know about having mares and geldings together," but Ralph didn't let the horses pause—they had to start moving around. At first they did so sort of chaotically, not really bumping into one another but coming close, throwing their heads, stopping suddenly, rearing a bit. But then, after not even five minutes, they coordinated themselves into a little herd. They started going around the arena, avoiding the jumps and easing through the corners but staying fairly close together, almost like a school of fish. Ralph and Andy kept them moving, and the more they moved, the more they seemed to sense what the others were doing. Along the fence, we were all staring at them.

Finally, one of the horses jumped a jump—it was Barry Boy, I saw by his blaze. Once he had done that, then the herd seemed to loosen up. The next horse to jump rather than go around was Curly, and then Curly jumped up onto the bank in the middle of the arena and jumped down. The bank now became rather popular—several of them jumped up and down. At one point two jumped on and then went down together, like a hunt pair abreast. I saw Andy move to guard the jump that was built into the fence at the end of the arena, an inviting coop. He didn't want adventurous horses to jump out.

What surprised me was how simultaneously relaxed and graceful all the horses were. One reason we were staring was that we thought they might hurt each other, but they organized themselves. Since Ralph and Andy didn't drive them, only directed them, the horses, I suppose, did not feel pushed and nervous. They were turned tactfully in big looping turns so that they would gallop in both directions. There was a kind of sinuousness to the way the herd moved, especially after certain horses began seeing jumping as easier than going around. And every time a horse jumped a fence on his own, all of us watching went "Oooh!" A voice beside me said, "They look so free."

It was Sophia.

She wasn't wearing riding clothes, just those pants tucked into her rubber boots, and a sweater and a raincoat. She put her hand in her pocket, and then she pulled out a Ritz cracker and put it in her mouth.

I said, "I love this."

In a minute or two, Ralph stepped into the path of the little herd and raised his flag. The lead horses—Pie in the Sky and one of the horses I didn't know—broke to the trot, and then the others followed. This part was interesting, too—at the trot, the herd fragmented, and the horses went off on their own. Then they were walking, and then Andy and Ralph headed toward them until they had bunched a little bit. But the Carmichaels didn't get too close, because they didn't want the horses to feel crowded. I thought it was amazing that two humans could make eight horses feel crowded.

Now Ralph waved his arm to us, and Jane said, "Okay, everyone get your horse and halter him, then tack him up." I glanced over at Dad, who was standing there smiling with his eyebrows raised. Then he saw me and sort of threw his hands in the air, as if to say, "What in the world, you learn something new every minute."

Pie in the Sky was blowing a little bit and his eyes were wide, but he walked right over to me and lowered his head for me to put on the halter. Then he walked along at my side as I took him over to the fence where the saddle and bridle were. Since Rodney had always cleaned him and tacked him up, I realized that I didn't have that sense of Pie in the Sky the way I did of my other horses: of looking at his head and standing beside him, and just getting to know him. I brushed off the last of the sand with my hand and patted him down the neck.

Sophia was standing beside my tack. She said, "Want me to hold him?"

I handed her the lead rope. She took it and tickled his nose with the end of it.

When we were tacked up, we still didn't mount. We walked around Ralph in a circle, cooling our horses while he stared at each of them in turn. After that he went over to Daphne and took Curly from her, and then he went over to Andy, who gave him a lasso. He mounted Curly and tossed the lasso around Barry Boy's neck. Barry Boy had a saddle on but not a bridle.

Now the six of us and our horses went and stood by the gate, while Ralph and Curly escorted Barry Boy over all the jumps in the arena and the bank. Ralph guided Curly with his left hand and his legs, holding the lasso with his right hand. I would say there was about twenty feet of rope between Ralph and Barry Boy—stiff rope, since they do something to a lasso to make it so stiff that you can push on it and loosen it if there's a cow or a calf at the other end. The loop is also stiff, so that it never really tightens around the lassoed animal. Anyway, Ralph and Curly cantered past the jumps and Barry Boy cantered over the jumps, and when they had done all of them, Andy raised them.

Since I had seen Ralph, Daphne, and Andy work before, I was pleased but not stunned. Everyone around me, though, seemed a little stunned. Sophia, now sitting on the railing near us, ate her crackers faster and faster. Dad was grinning, and Mr. Rosebury kept saying, "Well, I'll be a . . . Well, I'll be a . . . That is something. That is something." I guess Mr. Rosebury could not do anything without talking.

And in case anyone thought that Barry Boy was a special case, Ralph came over to where we were all standing and asked the girl from Santa Rosa if he could borrow her horse. She nodded.

He said, "How old is this one?"

"He's four."

"Breeding?"

She shook her head. "Don't know. We rescued him."

"Ever jumped before?"

She shook her head again.

"Well, let's get him started. What's his name?"

"Pinkie."

"What's your name?"

"Elizabeth."

Pinkie, you could see, was just a horse.

Ralph got off Curly and handed his reins to the girl, then tossed the lasso over Pinkie's head. Then he took off Pinkie's saddle and bridle and led him to the center of the arena, where he asked him to go around in a circle. Pinkie did this—he must have been lunged before. After a few minutes in each direction, when Ralph was sure that Pinkie was comfortable, he let Pinkie trot around him as he walked toward one long side of the arena where Andy had been setting up a crossbar. Now he started to run, having Pinkie trot over the crossbar. As he did so, Ralph popped up the rope so that it wouldn't catch on the jump standard. Pinkie did not recognize that he was supposed to jump, though—he just trotted through, knocking the poles aside. Ralph didn't respond. Andy reset the poles, and Ralph brought Pinkie around again. This time, Pinkie bent both knees and both hocks much more sharply in order to get his feet over the crossbar—you could see his mind working on this problem. He hit the poles and they flew away. Andy set the crossbar again.

This time, without Ralph doing a thing, Pinkie looked at the jump and then, three strides out from it, he picked up the canter and jumped it, bending his knees, lifting his shoulders, arcing the tiniest bit. If I had ever seen a horse solve a problem, this was it. Pinkie jumped the fence three times more, once as a crossbar and twice as a vertical, and each time he did it the right way. All the humans gathered around were laughing. It was that much fun to watch.

Ralph brought Pinkie down to the walk and led him over to his owner. She put the bridle on him and Ralph coiled up his lasso.

Now we all mounted up, including Daphne on Curly and Andy on Barry Boy, and Ralph did a funny thing—he sent us around the arena in a herd, getting the horses to do exactly what they had already done without riders, but with riders. I have to say that Pie in the Sky seemed to be enjoying this. He was as loose but also as organized as I had ever felt him to be. We went both directions, and even jumped a small jump because there was a horse on either side of us, and one went around the jump to the left and one went to the right, so we had to go over it. I can't say that this took Pie in the Sky by surprise—he was watching where he was going, and he prepared himself for the jump, jumped it, and went on. It was a small one, nothing like the big jumps we had jumped so many times. The best part about it was that Pie in the Sky was doing the thinking—understanding what the horses near us were about to do, and making up his mind accordingly.

The next thing Ralph did was divide us into two groups, sending our group to the far end of the arena. Now, at the walk, we had to weave in and out in a big circle, half of us going one direction and half of us going the other direction, and when we had done that for a while and the horses were cool and calm, Ralph said, "All right, folks. That's it for now. I want Curly, Norseman, Holiday, and Pie in the Sky right after lunch, and Pinkie, Riley, Parisienne, and Dalliance at three."

Ralph left. One by one, as our horses were cool, we went back to the barn. For the eight horses, I think there were now thirty or thirty-five spectators standing around, and I could hear them saying, "That looked like fun!" "The horses seemed to be having fun."

Daddy met me after I had jumped off Pie in the Sky and was leading him. We were about halfway between the arena and the barn. Daddy handed me a hot dog and said, "I think I learned something."

I said, "What?"

He said, "I don't know yet."

Chamois

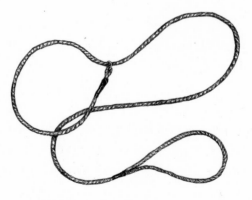

Lasso

Chapter 13

Sophia sat with us riders for lunch. She didn't say much, but in addition to her crackers and grapes, she ate some french fries. Really, none of us but Daphne said much. Daphne told the story of Curly and how his stall was right outside Mr. Pinckney's kitchen window. She said, "He looks in the window all the time, and even sticks his head in the window when he gets the chance. Mrs. Pinckney taught him to pull the cord to turn the light on and off. One time they overslept, and he got the window open and turned the light on and off to wake them up."

"I don't believe that," said the girl who was riding Dalliance.

Daphne shrugged and said, "Well, that's what they told me."

Two girls sort of shook their heads and rolled their eyes, but Daphne didn't pay attention. Sophia stared at her. I asked Nancy how Parisienne was doing. She said, "Not great. That's why she's here. My mom said we have to find another horse if Parisienne doesn't work out."

I said, "She's so pretty."

"I love her. But maybe she's too much for me. My trainer wanted me to get a different horse, but I couldn't resist her."

"How long have you had her?"

"Oh, a year now." She sighed. "I was headstrong."

Sophia said, "You have to be."

Nancy smiled.

Rodney had Pie in the Sky cleaned up for the afternoon session as though he had never been out of his stall, and as soon as Rodney gave me a leg up, Pie in the Sky tossed his head and started walking. Rodney said, "Ya givin' this boy a Guinness? He's lookin' forward to somethin'."

"What's a Guinness?"

"Food of the gods," said Rodney.

"Beer," said Sophia, coming up behind us.

"Yes, and you ask anyone, a nice draft is the holiest of nutrients," said Rodney.

As we walked along, Sophia kept her hand on Pie in the Sky's shoulder. She said, "What do you think you're going to do?"

"No telling."

"Was it fun this morning?"

"Well, it should have been a little scary, but it wasn't. Pie in the Sky was just having a good time. Ralph likes him."

She sniffed.

We were the last to arrive.

Over the lunch break, they had built a chute of five jumps that ran along the entire side of the arena and around the end, much longer than the chute we had built at the Marble Ranch. We didn't get to the jumping right away, though. First we had to warm the horses up, and Ralph let us do this on our own, watching us and then coming over to each of us and suggesting something or other. I was doing what I normally did with Pie in the Sky, bending, figure eights, getting him to step under. Ralph stood there, then said, "That horse know how to sidestep?"

I had Pie in the Sky step under.

"That's good, but I mean move to the side, crossing front and back."

"I don't think so."

"Well, here."

He stood next to my leg and used his hand and his flag to get Pie in the Sky to move sideways to the right. Then he said, "Horses don't want to move sideways. It isn't very natural or easy. But if you train him to do it and then have him do it, when he does it, he's saying, 'Okay, boss. I believe you.' This horse, there's just a little part of him that holds back, and that's the part that disorganizes him. He needs practice saying, 'Okay, boss. I believe you.'"

I nodded. Ralph went around to the other side and got Pie in the Sky to sidestep to the left. Ralph said, "Tomorrow we'll take ten minutes and work on that, okay?"

I nodded again. He patted Pie in the Sky on the rump and walked over to Norseman.

*   *   *

Curly, of course, was the first one through. In fact, as Daphne stood not far from the beginning of the chute taking Curly's bridle off, he was tossing his head and leaning toward the chute, and as soon as he was free, the little horse spun around and headed over the jumps. Every stride was perfect, and so was every arc. And even though Ralph had put a few scary things in there—a brush and a couple of chairs lying on their sides underneath parallel poles—Curly couldn't wait to get to them. At the other end, he turned around and came back, going straight to Ralph, who had shouted "Yup!" as Curly was coming over the last fence. Ralph gave him a lump of sugar. Then he said, "Now, this horse doesn't jump for the sugar—he just enjoys himself jumping. But he comes to me for the sugar when he's finished. Don't want him to gallop around and around with all these other horses waiting for their turns."

Next he threw Daphne into the saddle, and Daphne and Curly went over the jumps without a bridle. There were plenty of oohs and aahs from the crowd at this, and Sophia said, "Are you all going to do that?"

"Maybe. I hope . . ." I paused and thought, then said, "Not."

Ralph looked around and gestured me over. I led Pie in the Sky to him. He took Pie in the Sky, handed me a lump of sugar, and said, "You go down there and wait, and when he comes to you, you say 'Yup!' and give him that. Might take him a minute to come to you, but just wait. He knows you. He'll come to you, because everything about the chute is new and you are familiar."

I nodded and walked to the end of the chute. Now Andy

and Ralph picked up their flags, and Ralph stood Pie in the Sky at the beginning of the chute. Ralph let the horse go, and then the two of them waved him down the chute. He trotted to the first jump, hesitated, then jumped it. After that he got the idea—he trotted to the second jump much more smoothly, then cantered nicely over the last three. He came out of the chute cantering, saw me, trotted past, then came back. I held out my hand. When he came over to me, I said, "Yup!" and gave him the sugar. Andy was right nearby, and as I was petting Pie in the Sky, he put the lasso over his head and led him away, not forgetting to give me another lump of sugar.

The second time, Pie in the Sky was much smoother. He had the chute figured out and the sugar figured out. When Andy put the rope over his head, he said, "Okay. Now with you on him."

I followed them back to where Ralph was standing, smiling. He patted Pie in the Sky and said, "I told you this was a good one." I nodded.

I looked down the chute. Probably, I thought, it was easier than it looked. Probably—

Andy came over and laced his fingers to give me a leg up. Just then I heard Sophia say, "I want to do it."

You know the expression "music to my ears"? Well, the sound of her saying that was music to my ears. I turned around and looked at her. She was grinning. I said, "You sure?"

"It looks like so much fun."

I took off my hard hat and handed it to her.

Well, it was fun. It was fun to watch. She was only wearing slacks and rubber boots, but I had forgotten what a good rider

Sophia was, just as secure on a horse and perfect in her position as anyone I had ever seen. Had she really not ridden since August? You couldn't tell. As soon as Andy legged her up, she was right back where she had always been.

Except that she was not frowning.

Pie in the Sky turned and went down the chute, this time perfectly, and when they got to the end, I saw her lean forward and give him a lump of sugar. Then he trotted back, no halter or bridle, to Andy. Ralph went down the chute and raised the jumps, and then Pie in the Sky and Sophia went down it again, faster, bouncier, and happier. I laughed. We all laughed. It was only then that my heart sank just a bit, and I wondered if I'd made a mistake. Probably I would never ride Pie in the Sky again, and so never again would I know that exact feeling I'd gotten from jumping a horse that was so bright and proud and full of spirit. But he wasn't mine—that was evident just in the way Sophia's body moved with his. They were a pleasure to watch.

The lesson was interesting and exciting all the way through, so I didn't realize that Daddy and Mr. Rosebury were nowhere to be found. It was only when the four horses had cooled out (with their bridles on, of course), and were coming out the gate that I saw Mrs. Rosebury. Sophia didn't see her at first, either—she came over to me and gave me back my hard hat. But then she saw her mom and took Pie in the Sky over to her. Mrs. Rosebury patted Pie in the Sky's neck and gave him a kiss on the cheek. Yes, Sophia looked happy as could be, but Mrs. Rosebury looked relieved. I heard Sophia say, "Where is he?" and Mrs. Rosebury say, "Those buyers, the ones who wanted that property beside the golf course, made up their minds at the last minute, and he had to close the deal."

"Oh, good," said Sophia. I figured she meant it.

I didn't know where Dad had gone until about ten minutes later, when Parisienne and the others were getting ready for the second class, and Dad drove by with the trailer. I ran after him. He stopped in the loading area, and I saw that the hind end of the horse inside was gray. Or, you might say, Blue. I ran to the door at the front of the trailer and opened it. Blue nickered, then stuck his head out the door and looked around. I said, "We are going to have some fun!"

I untied the rope, and Dad put down the ramp and unhooked the chain. Blue reached out with his back foot, then made his way carefully down the ramp. When he was out, he lifted his head, pricked his ears, and whinnied. A horse in one of the barns whinnied back. Daddy took the lead rope from me and tied Blue to the trailer, then said, "We can get him ready right here."

He was already clean and damp—I guess Daddy had hosed him off at home—so all we did was brush him and smooth him over with the chamois. I put on my hard hat so I wouldn't have to carry it, and led him to the arena; Daddy would come along in a bit with the saddle and bridle. The whole time we walked over there, I petted Blue. He looked very beautiful, even compared to the expensive horses, and he minded his manners, too. He walked along beside me, never pulling or holding back. He knew this place very well. Time to show off a little.

This was the elementary group—Pinkie, Barry Boy, Parisienne, Riley, and Dalliance. Ralph had worked with the other four at least once, but never with Blue, so he came over and walked around him. I told him that Blue was seven, that he hadn't had much experience, and that he was nervous about jumping. Ralph just nodded. At one point, he held out his hand, and Blue arched his neck to sniff it. Yes, everything he did was elegant.

They had lowered the jumps in the chute and removed the third one, so there were two, then a galloping break of four or five strides, then two more. They were maybe two feet high. They had also set up two more on the other side of the arena on a circle, also quite low. The first thing Ralph did was put the lasso around each horse's neck and send him around the circle, at the trot or the canter—however the horse felt comfortable. If the horse wanted to keep going, the way Barry Boy did, he allowed that. If the horse didn't want to keep going, then Ralph used his flag to make him go until he went willingly. Blue went fourth. It took six times around until Blue went willingly. Ralph let him stop after seven.

The next thing was the chute, but they didn't go down it alone, like the more advanced horses had done. Barry Boy went first, with Pinkie, then Pinkie went with Riley, then Riley went with Dalliance, then Dalliance went with Parisienne, then Parisienne went with Blue, then Blue went with Parisienne again.

Of course, to me, these last two were the most interesting because they were almost the same size and rather similar-looking, though Parisienne was a bright bay and Blue was a dappled gray. But they had a similar stride and a similar jumping style, and Parisienne led the way by two strides, so their rhythm and their style over the jumps made it look like a circus trick—when she was going over the second fence, he was going over the first one, and so on, down the line. Daddy said, "I'll bet he likes that, having a girlfriend to do this with."

When Nancy and I had caught them and were walking them back to the others, we kept saying, "Oh, wasn't that great?" and "I just couldn't stop watching that!"

We did not have to jump them without bridles, but Ralph operated the same way as he had before—what the horses had done without us, they now did with us. We were to hold the reins but put our hands on their manes, take the jumping position, and go in pairs down through the chute. We went through three times each—my first two were with Parisienne, and my last was with Barry Boy. The jumps were still low. Blue was entirely comfortable with Parisienne by the time Nancy and I went through on them. He still let her be in front (which Daddy said was completely natural, since mares are in charge most of the time), and as we galloped down the chute, I felt as free as I ever had. Just as I had seen with the other horses, Blue handled all of the jumping—he adjusted the length of his strides, he decided where to take off, he positioned himself in relation to Parisienne. My job was to maintain my balance and go with him. It was easy, much easier than what I usually did with Blue, which was worry about all of it.

When we galloped through with Barry Boy, Blue was a little more forward. Blue did not really want Barry Boy to lead him by two strides, and I would have thought that would be scary, too, but it wasn't. By that time, he had been through the chute four times already. He was comfortable enough to play a little bit.

Ralph put the jumps up six inches.

This time we went through alone, and it was evident that height didn't matter, even to Pinkie. Jumping was an aspect of galloping. If they were galloping in a balanced, energetic, and attentive way, then jumping was easy. After we each went through twice, Ralph waved us over to where he was standing, and as we walked around him, he said, "Now, believe it or not, just about any horse can jump up to four feet or more, even Pinkie here. Curly can jump a course that is four or more inches taller than he is, and I've had a couple of puissance horses go over a foot taller than they were. The world record is eight feet and about an inch and a half. The horse who jumped that was sixteen hands, one inch. That means the jump was thirty-two and a half inches taller than the horse. But he has to be loose and he has to see that the jumping is his job. You can't be making all the decisions for him. You got to be quiet, and you got to be right with him. That's your job. Oh, and steering, but you can do that with your head."

We all laughed.

Then Ralph made us do the circle exercise. The first time around, we watched where we were going, and we all got around fine. The second time around, we were to look away from the track, and one by one, each of the horses galloped around the next jump and off to where we had been looking— I made myself look at the gate, and sure enough, we almost went through the gate. Ralph gathered us in the middle and said, "See, it doesn't matter why it happens. It only matters that now you know that it happens."

He didn't want to end on a bad note, though, so he had us get back on and jump a small looping course of four jumps, easy turns, first one direction, then the other. It was as natural as could be, just cantering and having fun. Then we untacked the horses and left them with Ralph. We took some apples that he produced from a bag, and walked to the far end of the arena, past where we had been before, maybe thirty feet beyond the end of the chute. When we were all gathered there and quiet, he sent the horses through the chute. They came with their ears pricked, their nostrils flared, and their manes flying. They looked graceful and free and happy. Barry Boy was in the lead, and Parisienne and Blue were right behind him, and they all came down to the trot and found us as soon as they were out of the chute. And all of us—Nancy, Andy, Elizabeth, Riley's owner, Mary, and Dalliance's owner, Linda, and I—we all petted them, gave them their apples, told them how wonderful they were, and promised them not only more apples but feed tubs full of carrots.

When we walked them around, cooling them out, everyone was smiling and talking, and telling everyone else what nice horses they had. It was not like a show at all.

By the time Blue was cool and untacked and we had all his stuff cleaned up and put away, it was getting dark, and by the time Daddy and I had loaded him up to take him home, it was really dark, and we were plowing through the forest with only our headlights showing the way. I always thought that was a spooky thing about the stables, that in spite of the golf course and all the houses around, you felt lost in the woods even driving down the road. I was pretty tired, and I just sat there most of the time, and even Daddy didn't say much, except "Ralph Carmichael is something of a horseman," but I could tell that he was happy and excited.

Finally, he heaved a sigh and said, "Well, now. What time are we supposed to be here tomorrow?"

I said, "Tomorrow is Sunday."

"Well, this . . . well . . ."

I looked at him. I said, "One lesson is enough, Daddy. We can skip tomorrow. I just wanted to try it." Then, after a long pause in the dark, I said, "I guess Sophia is going to be riding her own horse now."

"I guess so."

"Well, there you go." I didn't mean to say, "There you go," which sort of means "I told you so," but he didn't get mad at me for being sassy.

He just said, "Yup. There you go."

"Maybe, since Ralph and Andy and Daphne come here pretty often, we can do it again sometime."

"Maybe. I'd like to see whatever he does."

"I would, too."

But the fact was, I didn't mind missing the next day. For one thing, how could it be better than today? I needed some time to think about today, and everything else. To understand it, maybe, or maybe just to let it replay over and over in my mind. Another day, at this point, seemed like a whole sack of Halloween candy when you really just wanted to eat a few pieces of candy corn and enjoy them. Church would be a rest, listening to the brothers talk and the sisters gossip and eating something good—tomorrow was the Hollingsworths' turn, and they often brought a dish I liked, chicken fricassee with dump-lings. I dozed off and half dreamed, half remembered what those five horses looked like coming down the chute on their own, just because they liked it, just because they were with each other, just because they were horses and horses were born to move.

Lead Rope

Hay Bale

Chapter 14

SOPHIA DIDN'T COME TO SCHOOL ON MONDAY, BUT ON TUES-day she told Leslie, Stella, Gloria, Mary, and Luisa all about it. I didn't say much, just watched her as she smiled and talked and drew a picture of the chute on a page of her notebook. I had never seen her so bouncy. Gloria kept looking at me and saying, "You did this, too? Why didn't you call me?"

"We didn't know what was going to happen. Next time we will. I'll tell you when they come back."

"Where are they going?"

"Down south. Los Angeles."

"And she—"

"Daphne," said Sophia.

"And Daphne just goes to various schools?" said Leslie.

I nodded. Then I said, "They are not like anyone we know." I described that day on the bus when the paper wad flew and Daphne caught it without even looking, as far as I could tell.

Leslie said, "I want to watch, too. You know, there's this sport called pentathlon. You swim, fence, shoot pistols, run cross-country, and ride."

"What do you shoot?" said Stella.

"Targets," said Leslie.

"You are so weird," said Stella.

But she meant it as a compliment.

Dad didn't say anything about the clinic, and all Mom said was that the Carmichaels seemed like a very interesting family and she hoped to have them for supper sometime when they came back. But as the week progressed, I noticed that our arena started looking like a good place to lunge a horse over a few jumps and even make a chute, if only a small one. Daddy stacked all the jump poles in one place, and when I counted them, I saw that we had about sixteen. But I had another idea. On Thursday, I set up a fairly low jump right next to the fence, maybe two feet, and I gave it a very long wing on the other side, three poles end to end, maybe forty-eight feet.

I hung my tack on the gate and went to get Blue as if there were nothing special going on, then I brushed him off and brought him into the arena and let him go. Even though he had been out all night with Jack and the others, he was happy to play, and in the meantime, I fiddled with this and fiddled with that, pretending that his sniffing the hay bales and the cones and inspecting the jumps and my line of poles was not really my business. I did have the flag with me, and from time to time I waved it. At first, he took this as an excuse to bounce around and kick up his heels, but pretty soon he was just walking around, putting his nose under the fence, and looking here and there. When he came over to me the next time, I showed him a carrot. But I didn't give it to him.

Instead, I walked briskly over to the chute I had built, not paying any attention to him. He followed right behind me. I picked up the trot, and without looking at him, I jumped over the jump, trotted another ten feet, and turned around. Blue was on the other side of the fence, but when I waved the carrot, he hopped over it and came to me. I said, "Yup!" and gave him a piece of the carrot.

We did this about six more times. I would walk Blue around to the beginning of the chute and stand him there, then walk to where I had been standing before, stepping over the jump, and I would call, "Hey, Blue! Jump!" And lo and behold, here he came, trotting to me over the jump, looking for his carrot. It made me laugh every time.

When I brushed him and tacked him up, we went over the jump twice without doing anything else ahead of time—I wanted to do it while it was still in his mind, and he went straight over, no problem, seeming to enjoy it. Each time, I gave him a piece of a carrot. It wasn't until after I had gone on to other things like circles and transitions that I noticed Daddy watching. When we came up to where he was leaning against the fence, he said, "He seems to like that."

"Almost as much as I do," I said. But we didn't talk about it anymore. Daddy did leave the chute in place, though.

That night, Jane called. She told me that Melinda could not make her lesson Saturday, so Ellen would be there half an hour early, and asked if that was okay with me. Next she said that she didn't know if I would be disappointed or not, but Sophia had ridden every day that week and was signed up for a lesson on Pie in the Sky with the colonel Saturday. Since I would be there already, I was welcome to ride Onyx, if only hacking around. Sophia seemed to want the company. I said, "She should trailer him out here and ride with me. Onyx knows all the trails and they're really nice."

There was a pause, then Jane said, "I'll suggest that. I think she would like that. I think she should do that. I'll tell her dad."

I laughed out loud.

Then her voice got serious. She said, "Abby."

"Yes, Jane?"

"I have been thinking about our clinic all week, and I have to tell you one thing."

"What?"

"Ralph Carmichael is not like any horseman anywhere else that I know of. He does things his way, and he's been doing them his way for years and years. I would not, and I think that the colonel would not, send a herd of horses pell-mell down a line of jumps. Too much potential chaos. Ralph is able to control the chaos, but I'm not sure someone who didn't know his methods inside out could do the same. Do you know what I mean?"

I did, and said so. Then I added, "He'll be coming back. I won't do anything really weird until I take some more lessons from him."

"Okay," said Jane.

"But I got Blue to jump for a carrot today."

Jane said, "Well, dear, he is a carrot sort of horse rather than a stick sort of horse. That seems obvious."

After five days, I still felt good, though, and what good felt like was that I could think about Peter Finneran without grinding my teeth. I could see that he had his ideas, and they were meant to work in a certain way, and the real problem when I took Blue to his clinic was that Blue wasn't ready for Peter Finneran's ideas. He knew some things, but not enough things. Who had been prideful? Well, me, for one. Without knowing anything about what Peter Finneran was going to do, I expected to do it all perfectly, and for everyone to admire Blue, and me as well. Maybe I had been going to the clinic not to learn but to show off.

We all knew where that would get you.

And there was another thing about pride, I realized. If you were really having fun, then you didn't have time to be proud. I guess even Sophia had learned that. But even if she hadn't, she had had some fun, and I thought we both would always remember that better than we would remember the bad times.

That night, before I went to bed, I went out to check on the horses and give them a last bit of hay. When Blue and Jack came over to the fence, I said, "Let's start over. Whatever we do now, we do it because we like to do it."

Blue tossed his head, and Jack nickered, and I took those responses to mean "Yes."

About the Author

Jane Smiley is the author of many books for adults, including *Private Life*, *Horse Heaven*, and the Pulitzer Prize–winning *A Thousand Acres*. She was inducted into the American Academy of Arts and Letters in 2001.

Jane Smiley lives in Northern California, where she rides her horses every chance she gets. She is the author of three other novels for young readers, *The Georges and the Jewels*, *A Good Horse*, and *True Blue*, all featuring Abby Lovitt and her family's ranch.